Dare to Tease

Also From Carly Phillips

Dare to Tease

A Dare Nation Novella

By Carly Phillips

1001 DARK NIGHTS

PRESS

Dare to Tease
A Dare Nation Novella
By Carly Phillips

1001 Dark Nights
Copyright 2021 Carly Phillips
ISBN: 978-1-951812-41-6

Foreword: Copyright 2014 M. J. Rose

Published by 1001 Dark Nights Press, an imprint of Evil Eye
Concepts, Incorporated

Sign up for the 1001 Dark Nights Newsletter
and be entered to win a Tiffany Key necklace.

There's a contest every month!

Go to www.1001DarkNights.com to subscribe.

As a bonus, all subscribers can download
FIVE FREE exclusive books!

Acknowledgments from the Author

To Liz Berry, MJ Rose, and Jillian Stein, thank you for making me part of the 1001 family. It means more to me than you could ever know. You're the warmest, sweetest, most generous people and I'm so glad to call you all friends.

One Thousand and One Dark Nights

Once upon a time, in the future...

*I was a student fascinated with stories and learning.
I studied philosophy, poetry, history, the occult, and
the art and science of love and magic. I had a vast
library at my father's home and collected thousands
of volumes of fantastic tales.*

*I learned all about ancient races and bygone
times. About myths and legends and dreams of all
people through the millennium. And the more I read
the stronger my imagination grew until I discovered
that I was able to travel into the stories... to actually
become part of them.*

*I wish I could say that I listened to my teacher
and respected my gift, as I ought to have. If I had, I
would not be telling you this tale now.
But I was foolhardy and confused, showing off
with bravery.*

*One afternoon, curious about the myth of the
Arabian Nights, I traveled back to ancient Persia to
see for myself if it was true that every day Shahryar
(Persian: شهريار, "king") married a new virgin, and then
sent yesterday's wife to be beheaded. It was written
and I had read, that by the time he met Scheherazade,
the vizier's daughter, he'd killed one thousand
women.*

*Something went wrong with my efforts. I arrived
in the midst of the story and somehow exchanged
places with Scheherazade – a phenomena that had
never occurred before and that still to this day, I
cannot explain.*

*Now I am trapped in that ancient past. I have
taken on Scheherazade's life and the only way I can
protect myself and stay alive is to do what she did to
protect herself and stay alive.*

*Every night the King calls for me and listens as I spin tales.
And when the evening ends and dawn breaks, I stop at a
point that leaves him breathless and yearning for more.
And so the King spares my life for one more day, so that
he might hear the rest of my dark tale.*

*As soon as I finish a story... I begin a new
one... like the one that you, dear reader, have before
you now.*

Chapter One

"Today was one for the ages," Brianne Prescott said to her sister-in-law Quinn, her brother Austin's wife and his personal assistant. They all worked at Dare Nation, the sports agency her brother and uncle owned and where Bri was a publicist.

Quinn shook her head and laughed. "What was it you once told me? Athletes are like babies with big bank accounts?"

"And big dicks." Bri grinned at her own joke.

Quinn chuckled. "Considering I'm married to your brother, I won't comment."

But she'd insinuated it anyway. "Eww. Don't even make my thoughts go there," Bri muttered.

"Sorry," Quinn said, but she sounded more amused than apologetic. "Bad day?"

Bri nodded. "If it could go wrong, it did. I'm sure you heard about most of the fires I had to put out."

It was her job to keep the babies she'd mentioned in line, and for whatever reason, today had not been the day for good behavior. She'd had a client test positive for PEDs, one married guy accused of fathering a baby with an obvious gold-digger, and another who'd accidentally posted said big dick on Instagram, getting himself banned but not before the news had gone viral.

Quinn tucked a strand of her dark hair behind one ear and shook her head. "It makes you wonder what some of these guys are thinking."

"Amen."

Although Quinn knew firsthand what it was like to get involved with an arrogant former pro football player. Austin had come home one night to find a baby on his doorstep, and in a panic, he'd called Quinn. She'd moved in to help and never left, the two falling in love and Quinn taming the former playboy and becoming a mother to one adorable baby girl.

Wheeling her desk chair back, Bri stretched her legs with a groan. "All I want to do is go home, undress, pour myself a glass of wine, and relax." She glanced around the office she considered her sanctuary and sought peace.

The walls were painted turquoise, the shelves white. Her intention had been to give the room a beachy feel that would relax her during stressful times. Like now. Breathing in and out and enjoying Quinn's company, she began to chill out.

A knock sounded at her door, and Tara, Bri's secretary, popped her head in. "I'm leaving for the day. Do you need anything?"

"No, thanks. I'm good. Have a nice evening."

Tara smiled. "You, too. Oh! And you asked me to remind you to stop by the health clinic on the way home and take Braden the dress you borrowed from Willow."

Bri groaned at the reminder, and Tara rolled her eyes. "You forgot, didn't you?"

Both Quinn and Tara laughed, causing Bri to hold up her hands in defeat. "Hey, I knew I would. That's why I asked for the nudge!"

As Bri's second hand, Tara was used to Bri's never-ending lists and reminders.

"Night," Tara said to both Bri and Quinn before walking out.

"Guess I'm not going straight home after all," Bri said to Quinn. "Willow needs the dress for an event this weekend, and I had it cleaned after I wore it."

She glanced at the garment she'd borrowed from another sister-in-law, hanging on the back of her door. Willow was engaged to Bri's twin brother, Braden, a doctor at a downtown healthcare clinic and the team physician for the Miami Thunder football organization, where Willow worked as an athletic trainer.

"At least it's not as far as driving to the stadium to give it to Willow yourself," Quinn said, obviously looking for the bright side of Bri's never-ending day.

"True." Glancing out the window behind her, Bri noticed the sun beginning to set, the orange glow lowering on the horizon. "It's getting late, and I don't want to walk through that part of town alone after dark, so I'd better get going."

"Good point. I heard the clinic isn't in the best neighborhood, but Braden and Hudson are doing really good work."

"They are," Bri agreed. "And they seem happy with their jobs."

Hudson Northfield, Braden's best friend, also worked with both the football team and the health clinic. Tonight, Braden was at the clinic, but Bri wasn't sure if Hudson would be there as well. Hudson, with his dark brown hair, chocolate-colored eyes, and well-groomed beard, had become part of the family since he and Braden returned from a two-year stint for Doctors Without Borders, always at their gatherings and weddings.

But Bri didn't consider Hudson family. Not when she looked at him and her body parts tingled. All she could think about was how his facial hair would feel if he kissed her lips or started lower and that beard rubbed against her thighs. A tremor took hold, and she crossed her arms over her chest.

"What's that smile for?" Quinn asked, leaning forward in her seat.

Crap. Bri had been daydreaming about Hudson and probably grinning like a crazy person. "Nothing. Just thinking."

"About?" Quinn pushed, and when Bri didn't reply right away, Quinn jumped back in. "Could you be thinking about Hudson and the way he looks at you when he believes your brothers won't notice?"

"Why would you say that?"

And *did* Hudson look at her that way? Bri wondered. Yes, they had chemistry, but he'd never acted on it. Never given her any indication that he would, something she'd chalked up to Bro Code. Not making a move on his best friend's sister.

A broad smile spread over Quinn's face. "Look at that blush. You want him! I knew it!"

Bri shook her head. It didn't matter how she felt. "He's not going to act on whatever it is between us because of Braden, and I've come to terms with that." She pushed herself from her seat and picked up her handbag, determined to head over to the clinic before dark.

"Bri, wait." Quinn stood. "Look, I know you've had a rough time with men and relationships."

Raising an eyebrow, Bri did her best to withhold sarcasm as she replied. "Because they always want something from me like access to my agent brother or uncle or an introduction to a famous athlete. And once they get what they want, I'm expendable. Yeah, I haven't had an easy time." And maybe she was a touch bitter about it, too.

Quinn's expression softened. "Well, then you need to remember there's nothing Hudson needs from you, so if he won't make the first move, then maybe you should. Promise me you'll think about it?"

Bri walked past Quinn and lifted the dress from the hook behind her door. "I'll think about it." It was the best she could do.

A little while later, she was following Waze directions to the clinic, making sure she didn't get lost, despite the fact that she'd been there before. The farther downtown she drove, the more the buildings grew dilapidated. Graffiti covered much of the exteriors, and boys congregated in groups on street corners. She gripped the wheel tighter, and finally the female voice directed her to turn right and reach her destination.

She pulled her Audi into a gravel-covered parking lot and cut the engine. Braden's car wasn't within sight, and she'd kill him if he forgot to wait for her. Key fob in hand and bag slung over her arm, she exited the vehicle, then opened the back door to grab Willow's dress she'd hung on a hook and held it in one hand.

The moment she stepped onto the gravel, she cursed her high heels that wobbled on the pebbles beneath her.

"Hey, ma'am."

She spun at the sound of the male voice and nearly fell on her ass, but she managed to right herself. A stooped older man with a tattered jacket, too heavy for this time of year, stains on his tan pants, and ripped sneakers wove his way toward her.

"Got some money, pretty lady?" He came close enough for her to smell the alcohol on his breath.

She instinctively stepped back and fought to remain steady on her heels. Although a part of her was scared she was alone with him, another part felt bad. Who knew what circumstances led him to this point in his life? Still, she was torn between giving him money she feared might go for alcohol and turning him away. She opted to hope he used the cash for food.

She slid her purse down her shoulder so she could open it up and hand him money.

Taking her off guard, he grabbed for the bag. She jerked back, and her heels gave way. Her ankle twisted and she fell, her hands taking the brunt of her tumble as she slid, gravel digging into her palms and her hip hitting the ground hard.

The man bent over her, and she gasped, prepared to knee him in the balls if she had to, but before she could kick out, someone lifted the man by his jacket collar and pulled him away from her.

"Jimmy, back off," a familiar voice said. "You're scaring the lady." Hudson's brown eyes raked over her, concern etching his handsome features. "Are you okay?"

She nodded. "He just startled me."

Jimmy shuffled his feet on the ground, unable to meet Hudson's gaze. "I just wanted to help get the money she was reaching for." He pulled at his dirty shirt, his hands shaking.

Hudson scowled, and Bri had to admit even that glower was sexy.

"Well, that's not the way to handle someone offering to help you." He reached into his pocket and pulled out cash, handing it to the man. "Go get something to eat and quit bothering our visitors or I'm going to have to call the cops."

After grasping the cash like the lifeline it was, Jimmy walked away, muttering to himself, and Hudson turned his laser focus on her.

"Come on. Let me help you," he said in a gruff tone.

She glanced at her palms and winced. "Can you grab my wrists and pull me up?"

His gaze zeroed in on her hurt hands, and that ferocious expression deepened. "Yeah. Reach up," he said, but he glanced at her heels. "Kick those things off."

"Please don't leave my Louboutins." She couldn't believe she'd said that and blushed at the frivolous-sounding comment. "It's just they're a birthday gift from my mom."

His eyes softened at her admission.

Instead of pulling her up, he bent down and lifted her into his arms. "Oh! The dress. I came to give it to Braden for Willow." She pointed to the garment on the ground that, thank goodness, was covered in clear plastic.

"I'll send Nikki back out to grab it." He started toward the building, his hard body acting as a shield, protecting her from harm.

Not to mention, she inhaled how good he smelled, her face near his cheek, her hands laced around his neck, as he strode through the clinic entrance.

* * * *

Hudson held Bri close to his chest, his heart pounding out a rapid beat as he brought her inside.

He'd been doing paperwork in one of the back offices when the front receptionist called him to check out what was happening in the parking lot. It wasn't a shock to see Jimmy harassing people for money. The man never meant any harm, and Hudson didn't believe him to be violent, but seeing Bri on the ground had knocked the wind out of him.

Ignoring the arousing coconut scent of her hair tickling his nose and the feel of her supple body curling against him, he stopped at Nikki's desk. "Can you please grab the dress that fell outside? Jimmy was giving her a hard time, and she scraped her hands."

"Of course!" Nikki jumped up to head outside, and Hudson walked into a treatment room and placed Bri on the examination table.

Though reluctant to release her, he settled her and stepped back, looking her over from head to toe. Her dark hair fell around her shoulders, stray strands covering her cheeks.

He already knew her hands were in rough shape, but he wasn't sure about the rest of her. "Talk to me. Are you okay?"

She nodded. "I don't even know what happened. I went to give him money, he grabbed for my bag, and next thing I knew, I was on the ground." She extended her hands, palms up. "This is going to hurt, isn't it?"

He glanced at the abrasions and gravel stuck in the skin. "I'm afraid so, but I'll do my best to be gentle."

"I grew up keeping up with four brothers. I've had plenty of scrapes, and I can take it."

He laughed at her serious expression. "I know you can. Let me get everything I'll need, and we'll get you cleaned up. Does anything else hurt?"

"Other than my ego?" She grinned and shook her head. "My hip took the brunt of the fall, too, but I think I'll just have a nasty bruise.

Nothing that needs treatment."

She rubbed her right side, but he knew better than to ask her to lift her short skirt for a look. If he had to see what kind of panties she wore beneath, he'd be hard as a rock, and she'd notice. He'd gone to a lot of trouble to hide his desire for Braden's sister, but more than once, his best friend had called him out on it.

"Ice it tonight and tomorrow. Twenty minutes on, twenty off. And if it gets worse, we'll get you X-rayed," Braden said of her hip.

He opened the cabinets and removed items to irrigate the wound, clean out the gravel, put antibiotic ointment on, and wrap her hands in sterile gauze to keep bacteria out and prevent infection. Then he got to work, icing the area to numb it as best he could, cleaning and using a tweezer, carefully removing pieces of gravel.

Though she was stoic, he felt every wince and sharp intake of breath when he hurt her and was grateful when he finally soothed the area with Neosporin and wrapped her palms down to her wrists in order to secure the area.

After he'd cleaned up, he walked back over to where she sat, long, tanned legs dangling from the table, her precious black pumps with red soles tempting him. Fuck-me heels if he'd ever seen a pair, and considering his mother's taste and the fact that he came from money, he was familiar with the cost of those heels. Sexy, they had him envisioning Bri's legs wrapped around his waist, ankles crossed at his back, as he fucked her hard and deep.

He ran a hand over his face as if he could wipe away the erotic vision and reminded himself this was his best friend's sister. His twin. And though he had a hunch Braden would be okay with him dating his sister as long as his intentions were good, if things went bad, he'd lose not only his good buddy but a family he'd grown to love. One he needed because his father, in New York, was a selfish prick who liked to make demands and pull strings, more so since Hudson's older brother, Evan, had passed away suddenly last year due to an aneurysm that couldn't have been detected or prevented.

But there was no denying the woman on the exam table tempted him anyway. "How do you feel?" he asked.

"I won't lie. It's uncomfortable, but I'll be fine." Her forced smile did little to convince him she wasn't in more pain than she admitted.

"Don't lie to me. I know it hurts, but the best I can offer is Extra-

Strength Tylenol or ibuprofen."

She nodded. "If you have some, I'll take it now, please."

He left the room to get the pills and some water and returned, watching her take the meds. She put the empty cup behind her. "Thank you, Hudson. I don't know what I would have done if you hadn't shown up when you did."

"I've never known Jimmy to be violent, but he took things too far." He stepped closer and grasped her uninjured wrists in his hands, ending up between her spread thighs. "I'm sorry you got hurt."

Her indigo eyes met his, the unique color screaming she wasn't a Prescott but a Dare. Paul Dare was her biological father via sperm donation, something the Prescott kids had learned when Paul needed a kidney and he'd needed the children to get tested. Now that the truth was out, it was a shock nobody had realized the truth sooner based on eye color alone.

"I'm just glad I had you there tonight." Her gaze never left his.

He gripped her wrists tighter, leaning forward as if pulled by an invisible string, reeling him in, closer and closer to the woman and her tempting shimmering lips. Pulse pounding, he waited for her to stop him. For all the reasons he'd counted earlier, he almost wished she would. Because nothing but her saying no was going to prevent him from kissing her.

But her eyes gleamed with anticipation, and she leaned in until their mouths met and his world exploded. He tasted mint and Bri, a heady combination. One that surpassed anything he'd experienced before. His tongue slid against hers, and desire ripped through him, fast and furious, making him question how he could feel this much with just one kiss.

A soft moan escaped the back of her throat, and he swallowed the sound, nipping at her bottom lip. Her legs wrapped around his waist, ankles crossing. It was his dream come true except they were both fully dressed.

The kiss went on, hungry and full of desire until a sudden knock sounded on the door.

"I hear you rescued a damsel in distress." Before they could react, the door swung open and Braden stepped inside, his astute gaze sweeping the room and landing on first Hudson, then Bri.

And Hudson had no doubt they both looked guilty as hell.

Chapter Two

"What the hell did I just walk in on?" Braden's glare flickered over Bri, settling directly on Hudson.

"What does it look like?" Bri asked. "And before you go all big brother on me, I'm an adult, and I can kiss whoever I want."

She obviously wasn't about to let her twin push her around, and Hudson admired her spunk.

"You're in a public place," Braden said, sounding still pissed off.

"We're behind closed doors, and you didn't knock." Hudson stepped forward and put himself front and center. "Lay off your sister, Braden. We didn't do a damn thing wrong," he said, folding his arms across his chest. Braden might be his best friend, but he wasn't about to let him harass Bri over something that was none of his business.

Braden raised both hands in defeat. "Fine. I'll back off. You just took me by surprise. I don't want to see my sister lip locked with anyone, let alone my best friend." His frown epitomized every brother's reaction to walking in the way he had.

Bri walked over and placed her hand on Braden's shoulder. "Don't walk in when a door's shut and you won't see anything that might make you want to scrub your eyeballs."

His gaze fell to her hands, his eyes opening wide, obviously noticing her bandages for the first time. "What the hell happened? Are you okay?"

"I'm glad you realized what's important." She laughed and nodded. "I'm fine. Don't worry."

"Jimmy asked her for money, and when she opened her purse, he went to grab it," Hudson said.

"I pulled back and fell. Just a little road rash." She waved her hands in the air. "I'll live."

"The man's a hazard," Braden muttered.

"He didn't mean to hurt her, and you know it. We've treated him enough to know that his intentions are always good. That said, we should put installing cameras outside on our list of to-do things when we get the money to renovate this place."

"What kind of renovations?" Bri glanced from her brother to Hudson. Their eyes met, and sizzling awareness flashed between them, that kiss still very much on his mind and obviously on hers.

"Hudson and I have plans for this clinic if we can raise the funds we need. I'm going to talk to Uncle Paul this weekend." Braden's pseudo uncle/father was wealthy enough to fund his half of their plan.

Hudson's grandfather had left him a trust fund, but his father, Martin, was the trustee, and the chances of him giving him the money without strings were slim to none. Hence his upcoming trip to New York this coming weekend. Ever since Evan's death, his father's notion of continuing the family lineage with a grandchild had fallen on Hudson, and it was suffocating enough to prevent him from going home to New York after he left Doctors Without Borders. Now that he needed something from the man, Hudson was sure his parent would make him pay one way or another to get what he wanted.

"Well, you know I want details, but I'm too tired to focus on them now." Bri glanced at her hands. "Something tells me I'm going to have a tough few days getting any work done."

"You don't need to keep the gauze on. Just for a day or two. If you come back, I can rewrap it for you. Or if it's easier, I'll stop by," Hudson offered.

"Ooh, making house calls, Dr. Northfield?" She deliberately batted her eyelashes at him, and he grinned.

He liked that she could keep her sense of humor in the face of pain and problems. He liked that she could tease him even more.

Braden fake coughed loudly. "I'm still in the room."

With a roll of her eyes, she walked over and kissed Braden on the cheek. "Willow's dress is with Nikki out front. Tell her I said thank you and I'll call her soon."

"I will. Are you sure you can drive?" He gestured to the bandages around her palms and wrist.

She nodded. "I'll manage."

"Call me and let me know how you're doing, or I will track you down and hound you, and I know you don't want that." Leaning forward, he kissed her cheek.

"I'll walk you to your car." Hudson stepped forward and grasped her elbow.

Braden opened his mouth, probably to argue that he'd do it, but he took one look at Bri's face and caved. "Drive carefully," Braden said instead.

"I will," she promised her twin, no joking in her tone.

Glancing over his shoulder, Hudson met Braden's gaze. "We'll talk when I come back inside."

Hand on Bri's lower back, he led her out of the room, down the hall, and into the waiting area. "I'll be back," he told Nikki.

"Okay, Dr. Northfield," the receptionist said without looking up from her work.

The sun had set and the lights in the parking lot didn't all work. Dammit. He had to get the money from his father, because he doubted he could get the funding he needed from a bank.

He paused at the car and he heard the beep of her doors unlocking. A light reached them from the corner of the lot, and when she turned toward him, he glimpsed her pretty face in shadows.

"Thank you for everything tonight," she said, head tipped up toward him.

He smiled and brushed his knuckles over her cheek. "I'm glad I was here. Do me a favor?"

She lifted her eyebrows. "What's that?"

"Text me when you get home so I know you're safe." And he didn't mean he was checking up on her in a brotherly way, either.

"Okay." From the gleam in her eye, she obviously knew he was expressing interest.

What kind? What could they have together? He had no idea. Not yet. But he intended to find out.

* * * *

Hudson waited for Bri to drive away before he strode back into the clinic and headed to find Braden, who had settled into their shared office. Ever since they'd started working, the original head doctor, Thomas Anderson, had begun shifting more work their way and doing less on his end, just one of the reasons they were working on a takeover plan.

"Hey." Hudson pulled out a chair and dropped into it, the long day catching up with him.

Braden turned and glared.

"Knock it off," Hudson muttered. "It's not like I'm some asshole who's going to hurt your sister."

"You're not someone with serious relationships in your background, either." Braden's point was well made.

His romantic history was bland at best. He'd had women in his life but none who'd stuck or who he'd had any interest in pursuing a serious relationship with. Until Bri, but he wasn't going to share his feelings about her with Braden. Whatever happened between them was private.

"Trust me or not, but I'm not discussing her with you." Hudson kicked his feet up on the desk. "Want to order in dinner?"

After a long stare off, Braden nodded. He called in sandwiches from a nearby restaurant, and then talk turned to their plans to turn this run-down clinic into a state-of-the-art health center.

"Are you going to New York this weekend?" Braden asked, leaning back in his seat.

Hudson nodded. "My cousin is getting married, and we're close. I wouldn't miss it anyway, so I might as well kill two birds with one stone and talk to my father about releasing his hold on my trust fund."

"It's for a damned good cause." Braden gestured around them.

Hudson didn't need to look at the peeling beige walls, cracks on the ceiling, or old equipment to know his friend was right.

"I've never asked him for a cent for anything frivolous. I hope Dad takes that into account." But he knew his father didn't care about good deeds and helping others. He shrugged because he'd never understood his father and never would. "He and Evan were alike. Dedicated to the trading business and caring about things like family legacy and heirs. It sounds like a nineteenth-century drama."

Evan had been married, he and his wife trying to get her pregnant when he'd passed. TMI as far as Hudson was concerned, but that's how his family was. Trying to birth an heir to the fortune.

"I'm really sorry you lost him," Braden said.

"I know you are, and I appreciate it." It was different for his friend, Hudson thought. Braden was close with all of his siblings, whereas Hudson and Evan had been distant, not sharing things in common. "I miss the thought of him, but we rarely spoke, so I have some guilt tied up with it all."

Braden frowned. "You shouldn't carry that burden because you were different and didn't bond. Grieve? Of course. But don't feel guilty."

"I'm working on it." He swung his legs around and placed his feet on the floor and rose. "As far as our plan, we'll know a lot more after I go home this weekend." And he wasn't looking forward to the trip or the groveling he'd have to do in order to get what he wanted.

He worked a late shift at the clinic and finally locked up for the night. The warm Florida air hit him when he exited, but after two years in Brazil, he was used to humidity and heat. He climbed into his Ford SUV, turned on the ignition, and raised the AC, plugging in his phone and setting the music before pulling out of the lot.

He drummed his fingers to a current song on the radio as he drove toward the apartment he rented in the same building as Braden, when his cell phone rang and his father's name popped up on the screen.

Son of a bitch. Although he was tempted to ignore the call, his father would only try again later. The man was persistent, and Hudson had been ducking him lately, if only to give himself some peace.

He hit the button that accepted the call. "Hi, Dad."

"Hudson, I've been trying to get ahold of you," his father said in his typical annoyed tone, which came through the car speakers.

Hudson rolled his eyes. "I'm fine. How are you?"

"Your mother and I are fine as well, something you would know if you'd picked up or called me back."

"I have two jobs," Hudson reminded his father. "My free time is minimal."

"You wouldn't need to work those hours if you came home and took a job with Northfield International." The family international trading business that Hudson wanted nothing to do with.

He let out a low chuckle. "Are you forgetting you paid for medical school?"

"Yes, well, as you know, I had your brother to ultimately run the company then." Fate had disrupted Martin's plan.

To this day, Hudson didn't know how his father *felt* about the death of his firstborn son beyond the fact that he no longer had an heir to take over. Martin and Lucille Northfield thought they were nobility and treated everyone as a commodity that was either useful to them or not. For years his parents' attitude had suited Hudson fine because he'd been able to live life on his own terms. Now they needed him, and he wasn't about to give in.

"Are you coming home this weekend?" his father asked when Hudson didn't take the bait and answer the jab about his brother's death and Martin wanting Hudson to work with him.

"I'll be there," Hudson muttered.

"Good. I'm looking forward to talking about this further."

In other words, to harangue Hudson and try and change his mind. What he needed was a distraction, something or someone to shift his father's focus. Someone to keep Hudson busy and away from his family. His mind drifted back to Bri and that stunning kiss. It was more potent than anything he'd ever experienced, and he could have drowned in her and died a happy man.

"I'm bringing a date," he heard himself say.

And despite not knowing whether he could pull off the barely formed notion, he couldn't deny he liked the idea of taking Bri with him to the city. She was everything he'd just thought about and then some. A beautiful distraction to keep Hudson too busy to get pulled into endless conversation with his father except for the one about his trust fund. Not to mention, it gave him the opportunity to get to know her better away from her overprotective brothers.

His father began to cough, and Hudson waited for him to pull himself together. "You're what?"

Hudson frowned at the ridiculous question. His father had heard him just fine. "I'm bringing a date," he enunciated just to be sure. Though it wouldn't be easy, his cousin would add one to his table. Hell, she'd be thrilled he was bringing a date and had offered him a plus-one with his invitation.

"But what about Corinne? Surely you know she's excited to see you again after all this time," Martin said.

Hudson glanced up at the sky before shifting his gaze back to the road in front of him. "She's not invited to the wedding, and we haven't spoken in years," he said of a family friend's daughter his parents approved of as a match for Hudson.

They'd never dated, not for Corinne's lack of trying to corner him at events. His parents would like nothing more than a marriage within their social circle. It wasn't happening.

"Well, at least you're coming," his father said begrudgingly. "I'll let your mother know."

The bride knew he was coming, had known for months, but he'd let his parents wonder because then they wouldn't attempt to make plans for the weekend that included him and someone else ... like Corinne. And now that he was bringing a date, they wouldn't even try. At least he didn't have to worry about how his parents would treat his guest. They believed in good manners and appearances, and they'd treat Brianne with respect.

"I'll see you soon. Bye, Dad." Hudson disconnected the call just as he turned onto the street leading to his apartment.

Jesus, it had been a long day. He thought about what he'd just told his father and drew a deep breath, exhaling as he realized what he'd done.

Now he just had to convince Bri to join him for a weekend in New York. With his family. After sharing just one kiss.

Okay, so he had his work cut out for him, but he was up for the challenge.

* * * *

The next morning, Bri struggled to get dressed and ended up taking off the gauze on her hands since she'd all but ruined the wrapping anyway. The skin was raw and painful, and she gave up on a blouse with buttons and ended up in a pair of black slacks and a shirt she could pull over her head. Despite her love of high heels, she wasn't feeling all sexy and powerful, so she slid on a pair of ballet slippers instead.

Her hands throbbed, and she slathered on some Neosporin, but she didn't have Band-Aids large enough to cover the road rash, and by the time she was ready to leave for work, she was near tears in frustration. She'd really done a number on herself, and it wasn't going to be easy for a couple of days.

Her doorbell rang. She couldn't imagine who'd be here at this hour, but she went to the front door of her house and looked through the side window to see Hudson with a white plastic bag in his hand.

Looking sexy in his black Miami Thunder polo shirt and tan khakis, his beard well trimmed, she was reminded of what it felt like to have the soft hair rubbing against her skin as they'd kissed. She shivered, her nipples tightening beneath her bra.

"Shake it off, Brianne," she muttered as she unlocked the door and pulled it open. "Hudson! What are you doing here?"

"Making a house call."

Warmth spread through her at his thoughtfulness. "I guess that makes me special."

His answering grin seduced her right down to her toes, but when his gaze went to her hands, his smile turned to a frown. "From the looks of things, you could use my help."

She glanced at her greasy palms and winced. "Yes, I could."

He nodded. "The skin was pretty chafed last night, and I figured you'd need help with a fresh wrap so it doesn't get infected." He lifted the bag that obviously held medical supplies.

"Come on in." She stepped back, making room for him to enter.

He brushed past her, the warm, masculine smell of his cologne putting her into a sensual haze.

"Let's go into the kitchen," she said, her voice a shade deeper than normal.

As he walked ahead of her, he looked around, taking in her beloved home.

"From the day I saw this place, I loved it," he said. He'd visited recently for a family get-together.

"Me, too." Wanting a home of her own, Bri had bought the patio house last year.

She followed him to the kitchen, seeing the house through his eyes. Light blue walls with chair rails and molding painted in white, dark hardwood floors, and area rugs in strategic places with pops of color in various shades of blue. Her favorite color. A sense of pride filled her at knowing he liked her sanctuary as much as she did, which was odd that she cared what Hudson thought.

At thirty-two years old, she'd pretty much decided she might be on her own and not part of a couple, and she'd created the life she wanted without waiting for a guy to make her feel complete. She'd hired a decorator because she didn't have the time to pick things out for herself, described her taste, and ended up with everything she would have chosen anyway.

Hudson placed the bag on the counter near her barstools and began to take out gauze, tape, and Neosporin, which she already had. His thoughtfulness touched her.

Though Braden had texted to check in, it was Hudson who was here. "Thanks for coming over. I was struggling a bit." She wasn't one to ask for help and more the type to find solutions; still, she was glad he was here.

She settled herself on a barstool, and Hudson walked around the counter and came up beside her. "Since it looks like you did the cleanup and ointment, I'll just wrap it for you."

"I appreciate it." Holding out her hands, she waited as he began to wrap the gauze just as he'd done last night, finishing one hand with adept precision.

"So anything that you'll have to cancel thanks to the injury? Tennis? A workout? A date this weekend?" he asked, his gaze focused on his task as he casually tossed out possibilities.

Her heart stuttered on the last one. "A date?"

He lifted his head, his coffee-colored eyes focused on hers. "Yeah. Do you have a date this weekend?"

She blinked, her brain processing his question. "Are you saying I can't go out with someone because my hands are hurt?" Because that made no sense. Unless he was hinting at something more.

"That's exactly what I'm saying. Unless you go with someone capable of taking care of you." His fingers linked with hers, careful not to rub his bigger hand against her palms.

She tipped her head to the side. "Someone like you?" she prodded.

"Someone exactly like me."

That damned smile showed itself again, and her insides turned to mush. No man had ever had such a potent impact. "Are you asking me out, Dr. Northfield?"

Chapter Three

"I'm not only asking you out, I'm asking you to come to New York with me," he said.

Bri's eyes opened wide at the out-of-the-blue question.

"My cousin Serena is getting married, and I'd like you to go with me." He picked up the roll of gauze and started to wrap her other hand. "Serena and I are close. She's the one relative who completely gets that I want to do my own thing outside family expectations because she's the same way. She met her soon-to-be husband at the gym she works out at. He's a trainer. Suffice to say, her parents are paying for this wedding with gritted teeth."

Bri glanced at him in understanding. "Braden mentioned your family is..." She trailed off in search of words that sounded nicer than upper-class snobs and couldn't find any.

"Stuffy? Full of themselves? High and mighty with ridiculous expectations? Yes, that's them." He shook his head and laughed, but she heard the pain he hid beneath that forced sound and the wounded expression he couldn't completely conceal. "That's the drawback to attending, but there are perks, too." He finished bandaging her hand and put the gauze and tape on the counter.

"Oh, yeah? Name one," she said because she was seriously considering saying yes.

"Me. I'll be by your side."

Arrogant man, she thought with amusement. "Your cousin can add someone so close to the event?"

He nodded. "I spoke to her this morning, and it's no problem. Because she loves me." He raised his eyebrows and studied her.

"Well?"

Bri wasn't impulsive. She thought things through and went over the pros and cons in her mind. She just did it faster than most people, because in her business, she had to make split-second decisions to protect a player, fix a problem, or cover up a mistake. Where the press, paparazzi, and reputations were concerned, she often had to act quickly.

In this case, Hudson wasn't a stranger. She liked him, was seriously attracted, knew he kissed better than any man she'd met, and he wasn't using her for anything. The only cons were her annoying brothers, but driving them crazy was also sort of a plus in her mind. She and Hudson could have fun in the city, she'd learn about him without Braden interrupting, and she'd get to meet his enigmatic family and learn what made him tick.

"We'll be staying in a hotel and can get separate rooms if that's what's holding you back," he said in the wake of her silence.

She clasped his face between her hands – more like between her fingers, sparing her palms — and asked, "What if I don't want separate rooms?"

A sparkle lit his eyes. "Then I'll book one room," he said in a husky voice. "You're sure?"

"Are you trying to make me second-guess myself?" she asked with a teasing grin. She was already certain.

If just a kiss generated the kind of heat that kept her tossing and turning, what would a joining of their bodies do to her? She wanted this weekend for herself. She deserved it.

She hadn't been with a man in over a year, someone she'd chosen to scratch an itch, so to speak, and had learned her vibrator was a better choice. No one got too close. Not since the last relationship she'd had. Bri thought she'd been dating a salesman with no ties to the sports industry. In reality he'd wanted Damon to endorse a new energy drink his company was producing, and Austin, as Damon's agent, had already turned him down.

At that point, she'd shut down the idea of relationships and focused on herself. She had a feeling Hudson could decimate that self-made promise, but running the pros and cons, she didn't see a downside.

And when his lips met hers, she was even more sure. Just like last time, the kiss spiraled fast, their tongues intertwining, his hand coming up to grip the back of her neck and hold on tight.

She moaned and leaned into him, tasting a hint of mint and coffee, his hard chest pressing against hers, her breasts and hardened nipples rubbing against the fabric of her shirt. He lifted her shirt and slid his hands beneath the material, his calloused fingers sliding along her skin. Goose bumps prickled over her flesh, and arousal spread through her, thick and heavy.

Her head swirled, a buzzing noise sounding in her ears.

"Shit," he muttered, lifting his head. "My phone."

"Answer it," she said, knowing, as a doctor, any call for him could be important.

A regret-filled expression on his face, he pulled his phone from his pocket, drawing her attention to the hard erection tenting his pants.

"What?" Hudson's bark into the phone stunned her, and she glanced up, startled by the tone she'd never heard from him before.

"No, Dad, I'm not staying at the house. I'm staying at a hotel with Brianne." He paused, listening. "She's the guest I told you I was bringing," he said through clenched teeth.

She raised her eyebrows, and Hudson shot her an apologetic glance.

Apparently his father didn't approve of Hudson's plus-one if he was playing the *I didn't remember game*. She'd known their relationship was difficult, and now she was seeing how it affected Hudson firsthand, the stress his father caused just by hearing his voice or asking questions.

"I can't talk now, Dad. It's a bad time. Tell Mother I'm sorry I'm not sleeping at the house, but I'll see her this weekend. Goodbye." He disconnected the call and shook his head, the sensual mood between them obviously gone. "Sorry about that. I told you my father's a pompous jerk."

"Hey, I get it. The man who raised me was a tough man." And that was putting it mildly.

Hudson's gaze softened. "Braden's told me."

"Yeah. The boys had it bad, but Jaxon and Braden took the brunt of his disdain." She swallowed hard, hating to remember the yelling and belittling that had gone on in the house while she was growing up. Her mother would beg her father to stop, and he'd go harder on the boys. Never physical abuse, but the mental anguish was bad enough on their self-esteem.

Hudson leaned against the counter near her chair. "Because Jaxon chose baseball over football and because Braden was too smart and not athletically inclined."

She drew a deep breath and nodded. "Yeah. And he basically left me alone. But this is about you. Are you okay?"

"Yes. He's only getting to me because I need something from him, but we can talk about that on the way to New York. Right now I'd rather forget about my old man if that's okay with you."

"It is." Because he'd promised to fill her in, she had no problem letting the subject go for now.

"Do you want to bail on me now?" He drew himself up straighter as if waiting for the blow.

She grasped his hands with her fingers. "Considering how I was raised and the athletes I deal with on a daily basis, do I look like a woman who can't handle a difficult man?"

His easy grin returned. "I forgot who I was dealing with. You can handle anything and anyone."

Apparently they weren't including the incident with Jimmy last night, for which she was grateful.

She grinned. "I certainly can. And that includes you."

He tipped his head back and laughed. "If I didn't mention it, the wedding is formal."

"Got it." She'd have to go dress shopping. Of course, she had a long gown or two in her closest she could wear, but she'd rather buy something new for the occasion. Something that made a statement and had her date drooling. "I take it that means you're wearing a tuxedo?"

He nodded.

Which meant she'd be doing some drooling of her own.

* * * *

The next morning, Bri walked into her favorite boutique and was immediately surrounded by gorgeous dresses in stunning colors and varying hues. Some sparkled, others glittered, and many were solid, the designs speaking for themselves.

Hudson had texted her a general itinerary for the weekend, which included a family dinner Friday night at his parents' house, no wedding obligations since he wasn't part of the bridal party, and the wedding would take place on Saturday evening. Since Bri had appropriate clothing for the night with his parents and the rest of the weekend was casual other than the event itself, she didn't need to shop for anything else.

She'd asked where they were staying and made a Glam Squad appointment for hair and makeup, and Hudson had promised to disappear from the room while she got ready. Her entire point was to look spectacular, and she hoped he liked and appreciated the end result.

She was perusing the dresses, waiting for her best friend and sister-in-law, Macy, to arrive and help her choose. She'd met Macy at an exercise class in their local gym, and they'd been friends ever since. She'd also married Bri's brother Jaxon in what started out as a marriage of convenience and ended up with them head-over-heels in love. So now Bri had her best friend as her sister-in-law, and she loved that Macy was family.

A bell rang, indicating someone had entered the store, and Bri glanced up to see Macy walking toward her. Because she owned a website design business and worked from home, Macy could make her own hours, and Bri's last-minute request to shop wasn't a problem for her.

"I'm here, but I still don't know why you need a formal dress." Macy, her hair pulled up in a casual bun, wore a pair of leggings and a floral tunic top and looked relaxed and happy, a far cry from the panicked woman she'd been when she'd married Jaxon to help her keep custody of her teenage sister.

Bri held up a raspberry-colored gown with what looked like silver clasps on the tops of the shoulders. "Because I'm going to a wedding in Manhattan this weekend. Oh, and I also need shoes, so plan on a long day. Does this color go with my complexion?"

Macy shook her head. "I don't love it. Let's keep looking. And don't keep me in suspense. This has to be a last-minute trip or you'd have mentioned it sooner. Not to mention have already gone shopping. So what's going on?"

Her friend knew that Bri rarely dated and wasn't big on one-night stands, either, so this news would come as a shock. One she'd wanted to tell Macy in person because it would lead to a long conversation, and Macy had been in a rush when Bri had called her to make plans. She'd only had time to tell her the story about falling and hurting her hands before they'd agreed on a time to meet.

She figured she might as well start at the beginning. "Hudson and I kissed. Twice."

"What?" Macy's raised voice caused other customers to turn around and an uppity saleswoman to frown at them.

Bri grinned, ignoring the woman. "After I fell outside the clinic, I couldn't stand up in my heels. Hudson carried me inside and took care of my palms. I thanked him, one thing led to another … and we kissed, but Braden interrupted us."

"That must have gone over well." Macy's voice dripped sarcasm because she knew how protective the Prescott brothers could be. "And the second time?" she asked.

"Yesterday at my house. He came by to check on me and brought medical supplies to bandage my palms."

Although he'd wrapped her hands again, before he'd left, he'd shown her the large bandages she'd have an easier time applying on her own, and she'd put the less obvious dressing on her hands today. At night he'd instructed her to let the wounds breathe and leave them uncovered.

"He asked me to be his plus-one this weekend at a family wedding, and after I agreed, we kissed. Again."

Macy let out a low whistle. "A *family* wedding? Isn't that like making a serious statement or something?"

She shook her head. "No. In this case it's more like he's letting his family know he's living his own life and to back off, don't matchmake or pressure him to come home in any way."

"Aah. And what does his invitation say to you?" Macy asked. "Or better yet, what does your agreement say to him? Is this a serious thing?" Macy's question was a valid one.

Bri's feelings about dating and being used or hurt hadn't changed, but she couldn't deny the flutters in her stomach when she so much as thought about Hudson, either. She also understood he needed her as a buffer with his family, but she knew that going in, which made the situation understandable, and there were no feelings of being exploited for her connections or used in any way. She liked the idea of helping him out and making this weekend easier for him.

"Well," Bri said, picking up a sleek long black dress. "I don't know Hudson's views on relationships, but I know mine. And this is a weekend away with a sexy man and the chance to explore things without all my brothers butting in." She shrugged. "That's about as far as I've thought things through. In other words, we're going to a wedding, not getting married. It's all good."

Macy smiled. "Well, you're excited, and that's enough for me. Now let's pick a dress."

They sorted through the possibilities and chose some for Bri to try on. There was one large fitting room in the back, and Macy came in with her, talking as Bri tried on one gown after another.

"Do your brothers know about your trip this weekend?" she asked.

"Can you zip me?" Bri turned, lifting her hair so Macy could pull up the zipper in the back. "I certainly haven't told any of them," she said, picking up the discussion where they'd left off. "I'm not hiding it, but I don't need to either get into an argument about my personal life or have them give Hudson a hard time because he's doing whatever with their sister." She made a face that expressed what she thought of their interference.

"You do realize Braden is the one who gives Hudson the weekend off from the team? And they work together at the clinic, so he'll know Hudson is away. And he'll realize you're gone, too, and put two and two together."

Bri rolled her eyes. "Whatever. He'll get over himself. We're all adults, and when this thing, whatever it is, with Hudson ends, we can all stay friends."

She ignored the twinge in her stomach at the thought, be it of things ending, which was silly when they'd barely begun, or just being Hudson's friend. She shook her head, knowing she was being ridiculous. They were friends before they'd kissed, and they'd be friends after they slept together. Case closed.

"I love that dress on you!" Macy exclaimed.

Bri glanced in the full-length mirror, taking in the rose-gold, embellished, lace-embroidered, illusion gown with a low vee in the front that was flattering yet classy. The lace hugged her curves on top but fluttered beautifully at the bottom.

"Oh, look! There's a matching scarf to drape over your shoulders." Macy picked up the piece that had fallen to the floor and handed it to her.

"I love this," Bri said, smoothing her hand over her hip.

She'd make a statement in this gown while keeping in style and not give Hudson's parents anything to complain about. Other than her lack of pedigree, she thought wryly.

Macy clapped her hands. "Yay! Perfect choice. Now we go shopping for shoes and a small purse?"

Bri nodded. "Just as soon as I pay."

She'd seen the price on this dress, and by the time she bought the shoes and bag, she'd have a hefty credit card statement next month. Even with her generous salary, this was a big hit.

She glanced in the mirror one more time. Her dark hair and tanned skin provided the perfect contrast to the lighter-colored gown. If Hudson's chocolate eyes darkened at the sight of her in this dress, the money would be well spent.

* * * *

Hudson had his suitcase open on the bed, his tuxedo hanging on the door waiting to be placed inside the garment bag. He'd actually had to buy a tuxedo for the wedding because his clothing consisted of khaki shorts and collared T-shirts from his time in Brazil. When he'd moved to Florida, he'd purchased pants for clinic and stadium work. Not a formal or overly dressy item could be found in his closet, and though his mother would be horrified, Hudson liked it that way.

He added his Dopp kit to the suitcase, zipped it up, and rolled the bag near the door. He was about to turn around and grab his tuxedo when a knock sounded.

He swung open his door to find Braden standing outside. "Hey, come on in."

Braden strode inside, his gaze going to the carry-on. "Ready to go?"

"As ready as I'll ever be to deal with the family."

Braden made himself comfortable, dropping onto the leather couch Hudson had splurged on. "Are you looking forward to the wedding at least? I know you haven't seen Serena in a while, and you two are close."

Joining him, Hudson sat down on the opposite end of the sofa. "That's the one thing I'm excited for. She deserves to be happy."

Braden nodded. "Where are you staying?"

This was starting to feel like twenty questions, Hudson thought, narrowing his gaze. No, he hadn't told Braden he was taking Bri, but there was every chance Braden already knew and was testing him, in which case he had no problem playing the long game and making his friend work for the answers.

"I made a reservation at the Four Seasons." In fact, he'd pulled family strings, and he'd managed to book them into a suite. He wanted to make a good impression with Bri.

Folding his arms across his chest, he met Braden's gaze and waited for the explosion.

Braden raised his eyebrows. "I hope you mean you made reservations, as in plural?"

"None of your business, and I take it the family grapevine is alive and well?" Hudson asked with a grin and heard the grinding of his friend's teeth.

The last time he'd seen a scowl that deep on Braden's face was during a walk through over-one-hundred-degree heat to a village that was a few miles away after their Jeep had broken down.

"Bri went dress shopping with Macy. She told Jaxon, and Jaxon told me. I can't believe you weren't going to mention it," Braden muttered.

He leaned forward in his seat and met Braden's gaze. "Look, she's your twin. I get that you're overprotective, but this is me, okay? I'm not going to hurt her."

"You'd better not or you'll have four Prescotts to answer to."

Hudson was smart enough not to reply and to let his actions speak for him.

Chapter Four

Hudson said he'd pick her up by noon on Thursday, and Bri was ready when a town car pulled into her driveway. Both the driver and Hudson exited the vehicle, but she couldn't tear her gaze from her date for the weekend.

Wearing a pair of jeans and a crew-neck shirt, aviators covering his eyes, Hudson strode toward her, looking sexy as hell.

He met her at the bottom of her front steps and glanced at her bags. "It's one weekend," he said, taking in the largest suitcase she owned, a carry-on for her toiletries and personal items, and the tote she always carried with her when she traveled.

"Well, hello to you, too." She grinned and lifted the handle on the luggage, pulling it higher so she could drag it behind her when she walked.

He smiled and brushed his lips over hers. "Sorry. Hello. You look great." His gaze raked over her, and though she wore a simple outfit, a pair of jeans, a white T-shirt, and a casual black blazer with sleeves that easily pushed up on her arms, from the heat in his eyes, she might as well be naked.

"Thank you. And as for the bags, I'm a woman. Enough said."

He chuckled and took the luggage from her hand. "I didn't have sisters. I wouldn't know the drill."

She wasn't about to ask him about past girlfriends who'd made themselves at home in his apartment. She didn't want to know, but one thing was certain. After sharing a bathroom with her this weekend, he would definitely learn.

He handed the luggage to the driver, who loaded the trunk, and they headed to the airport. Hudson had splurged on first-class, and the trip to New York was as fast and easy as their conversation. He was interested in her job and what she did for her clients on a daily basis, and she was only too happy to fill him in on the details, omitting names where the stories and history weren't public knowledge.

They sat side by side as they talked, and he couldn't stop laughing at some of the shenanigans the guys got themselves into.

"But crises don't occur every day, so mostly my job is to keep them in the spotlight in a positive way. I build their brand both inside and outside their sport and make sure community goodwill is a priority. Good press is always a bonus. And if they have an overall solid reputation, they can draw on that goodwill in times of trouble." She handed her glass to a passing flight attendant and turned back to Hudson. "If a guy is an overall jerk and then goes on to do something stupid, nobody will cut him any slack, and the athlete won't deserve any. Even if he is my client."

"You love your job." Braden studied her with admiration and true attentiveness she rarely saw in a man when it came to her profession. Unless, of course, it provided an opening for something they needed.

She shook those thoughts out of her mind and refocused on the man next to her. As much as he was curious about her, she wanted to know more about him.

"I do love it, and I know how lucky that makes me. Not everyone can get up in the morning and do something they enjoy." She tipped her head, leaning against the seat behind her. "What about you? Do you love your job? Or should I say jobs?"

"Hmm. Good question. I like the job with the Thunder. It moves fast on game day, and I get to watch a player from injury through to recovery, which makes it satisfying, though I haven't been on board long enough to see anything substantial. And thank God for that."

She nodded in agreement. Nobody wanted an injury to happen to any player in the game. "You said like, not love."

"I loved what I did with Doctors Without Borders, though one stint really was enough for me. I'd rather be in the States and do a form of humanitarian work here. Which is why I chose the clinic. The pay from working for the Thunder lets me work for free at the health care center."

This was the part of Hudson Northfield that drew her to him.

Yes, the outside packaging was pure sex appeal, but the man inside was a kind, decent man who cared for others despite the fact that he could have gone into his family's business and helped to make them more money.

"What are you thinking about?" he asked.

Their faces were close together as they spoke, creating a bubble of intimacy and making it easier to be honest. "About how much I admire you. How you could be on the money train with your family in New York, but instead you're all about giving back. I like that about you." She studied his expression and the look in his eyes. "What's wrong? Something's bothering you."

"You've come to read me well in a very short time," he said on a low chuckle. "I do have an issue to deal with while I'm home."

She reached out and clasped their hands together. Her palms felt better now that it had been a few days since she'd fallen, and the bandages made it easier to do things. Like hold hands. "I'm a good listener … if you want to unload your problems."

He hesitated, obviously weighing his words. "You know the plans for the clinic Braden mentioned the day he walked in on us?"

She nodded. In the rush of her sudden trip, buying a dress, packing, and making sure her clients were covered by another PR person if she wasn't reachable, she'd forgotten to ask either man about it since.

"Braden and I want to renovate and remodel the clinic into a state-of-the-art place where people who don't have access to insurance or good care can still come in and get treated. As it stands now, the equipment is old, the building run-down, and it's hard to entice professionals to come work there."

"I love that idea!"

"Obviously so do I. Braden's going to talk to Paul Dare about funding, and I need to have the same conversation with my father. My grandfather left me money in trust, but he also made my father the trustee, and it's at his discretion whether or not to let me have money from the principal."

She realized he'd begun tapping a foot against the floor, his knee bouncing up and down with every contact. "You're really wound up about this, aren't you?"

He nodded. "My father, Martin, isn't known for his altruism

unless it makes him look good within his social or business circles. He's not going to easily fund a clinic just because I ask him to. It would be so much easier if my grandfather had released that money when I hit a certain age." He shook his head and groaned. "But he didn't, and that's that."

"I'm sorry." She couldn't imagine what a hit to his pride it would be to have to ask his father for anything. "It sounds like you have a difficult relationship." She bit down on her lip then asked, "Why is that?"

He groaned. "Because I had no interest in the family business, and as long as Evan was alive, that didn't matter. He let me to go medical school and live my life on my terms because Evan was filling the requisite oldest-son role." His hands squeezed tighter around hers. "Now he wants me to give up my life, come home, and pretend to be someone I'm not."

Now she understood why asking his father about releasing funds on a new business venture that kept Hudson in Florida and not in New York, where the man could pressure his son into doing his bidding, would be even more difficult.

The flight attendant's voice sounded on the loudspeaker, letting them know to prepare for landing.

Bri checked her seat belt and glanced at Hudson. "At least I'll be there for backup or a distraction," she said with a cheeky grin, unsure of what else to do or say in the moment.

Lifting her hand, he pressed his lips against the top of it, and her skin tingled, her body responding to that small gesture.

"Let's not dwell on it," he said, shaking off the black mood that had descended while he explained his situation. "I'm in New York City with a beautiful woman. We came to have fun, and that's what we are going to do."

She beamed from his compliment and looked forward to what the weekend had in store.

* * * *

Hudson waited in the outer room of the suite while Bri changed and put herself together in the bedroom and bathroom area. Though she'd all but warned him he didn't know about women and travel, he was stunned when she unpacked everything in her carry-on. Thank God the bathroom had a sitting area, because the woman had more makeup than he'd seen in a department store as he walked through to find the Men's Department.

He'd had relationships, but none had reached the point where he'd wanted anyone's clothing or toiletries stashed at his place. To him, that sent the wrong signal, and until Bri, there'd been no woman who'd tempted him to take things further than a date or two or a one-night stand. So here he was in a luxury hotel suite, surrounded by feminine bottles, makeup, and clothing, and he didn't mind one bit.

He straightened his black sport jacket he'd paired with black slacks and a light blue dress shirt, forgoing a tie. His father might be in a business suit, but that wasn't Hudson's way, and he wasn't going to bow to his father's rules just because he needed something from the man that was rightfully his to begin with.

He passed by the room bar, deciding not to drink before he had to deal with his parents, no matter how much he wanted to take the edge off first. Striding to the window, he looked out over Central Park and the Manhattan skyline, the view always stunning, and wished any time he visited the city he could relax and enjoy it instead of being stressed and uptight.

After confiding in Bri on the plane today, he'd immediately felt lighter for sharing the heavy burden he carried, wanting to meet Braden on equal ground when they began work on the clinic. Her presence went a long way toward calming him, and he decided to look at her any time his father twisted the guilt-laden knife.

The sound of Bri clearing her throat alerted him to her presence, and he turned to see her standing in the center of the room, waiting for his reaction. No question, she knew not only how to make an entrance but how to make a statement.

She wore a white sleeveless sequined pantsuit that fitted her perfectly but remained classy. A V-neck bared her tanned skin but not the breasts he'd yet to see in person or feel in his hands. The bottom of the pant legs were wide, her silver shoes high, and she clutched a matching sparkling bag beneath one arm, a silver shawl hanging over her other one. Her dark hair flowed in perfect waves around her face, and her makeup was flawless.

She simply took his breath away. "Jesus, Bri. You're gorgeous."

Smiling and eyes twinkling, she said, "Thank you, but you haven't seen the best part." She slid her hair over one shoulder and pivoted, turning her back to him. Thick straps crossed her tanned back, and the material came to a V at a low but modest point where the pants began.

"How the hell do you expect me to concentrate on what anyone says at the dinner table?" All he'd be thinking about was bringing her home, peeling that pantsuit off her perfect body, and burying himself deep inside her wet heat.

She spun back to him. "I told you I'd be your distraction, didn't I?"

He let out a low groan, resigning himself to a long, uncomfortable night, both with his parents and thanks to his now hard dick, before they returned here to make use of the king-size bed in the other room.

* * * *

Bri hadn't been raised in a wealthy home, but between Uncle Paul and the athletes she now represented, she knew how to handle herself. Neither status nor people with attitudes scared her, yet she had a feeling Hudson's parents would test her resolve. Once again in a town car with a driver, she and Hudson pulled up to a home in Greenwich, Connecticut, hidden by dense trees, at the end of a long driveway that was nearly invisible off the main road.

"Did you grow up here?" she asked of the mansion in front of her with ivy growing over the brick façade.

He nodded. "I did."

Though he looked extraordinarily handsome, she noted he'd grown more and more silent as they approached their destination, and she'd left him to his brooding thoughts. There would be time enough to coax him back to his smiling self when they returned to the hotel.

The car came to a stop at the front of the house on a circular driveway, and the driver opened the door for her to climb out.

"I'll be here when you're ready to leave," the man who'd introduced himself as Tom said.

"Thank you. I'm not sure how long we'll be." Hudson nodded at the driver.

Placing a hand on her bare lower back, he led her up the steps and rang the doorbell. If it was her mother's house or even Uncle Paul's, if they knew she was coming, the door would be unlocked and she'd let herself inside.

She drew a deep breath just as the door opened and what she assumed was a maid greeted them. Middle-aged, hair pulled back in a bun, she was the stereotypical greeter one would see in a movie except this was real life. Hudson's life.

"Hello, Dr. Northfield. Welcome home."

"Hi, Maggie. And please call me Hudson. I ate milk and cookies in the kitchen and told you about my day after school."

The woman's expression softened. "Yes, you did. And who is this beautiful young woman?"

"Brianne Prescott, this is Maggie. Maggie, meet Brianne."

Brianne treated the woman to her warmest smile. "Hi, Maggie. It's a pleasure to meet you."

"The pleasure is mine. I don't see Dr. … Hudson often anymore, and it's nice to know he's not alone."

"Maggie, is that Hudson?" a woman's voice called out.

"If she was so curious, she could have met me at the door," Hudson muttered, and Bri placed a hand on his arm to calm him.

Maggie stepped back, and they walked inside. Marble floors, a winding staircase to the left, and heavy dark wood décor and equally dark drapery on the windows surrounded them.

"Hudson, it's about time you came home!" His mother, an attractive woman with dark hair and a Chanel skirt and jacket, came forward to greet him. She possessed glowing skin and a perfect bob surrounding her made-up face.

"Hello, Mother." Hudson duly offered up his cheek, which she air-kissed. "And you must be Brianne." She offered her hand, and Bri took it.

"So nice to meet you. Hudson's told me such nice things about you and the family."

"Has he now?"

Hudson cleared his throat, and Bri did her best not to poke him in the side.

"Come. Your father's waiting in the study. We can have drinks before dinner." She turned and walked away, fully expecting them to follow.

"Do you want to run yet?" Hudson's lips twitched in a grin.

"Nah. It'll take more than a cool breeze to scare me. Let's go. I'm curious about your father."

Hudson rolled his eyes. Hooking his arm in hers, they headed the way his mother had gone, and soon Bri found herself in a wood-paneled room with built-in bookshelves and what appeared to be old books lining the shelves. An antique clock hung on one wall, and a large mahogany desk took up one side of the room.

A man in a suit stood beside a bay window, turning when they entered. Bri stared at an older version of Hudson. Martin Northfield's salt-and-pepper hair extended to his beard, giving her a glimpse of Hudson's appearance in the future. Even their dour expressions were similar. She much preferred his laughing persona and the sexy grin that tempted her to sin. She doubted she'd see that smile on his father's face tonight. Hudson's, either.

"Hello, Dad." As Hudson spoke, he pulled Bri closer to his side.

"Hudson. It's good to see you." He stepped forward and shook his son's hand.

Bri did her best not to react, although at this point, she really wanted to cry for the cold atmosphere in which Hudson had been raised. She applauded him for managing to escape and become the kind, caring man she knew him to be.

"Dad, this is Brianne Prescott. Brianne, my father, Martin."

"It's a pleasure to meet you, Brianne." His father looked her over and, seemingly satisfied, gave her a nod. "Can I get either of you a drink?" he asked.

Hudson glanced her way, but she shook her head. "No, thank you." Alcohol made her tired, and she wanted to be wide-awake for Hudson later.

"None for me, either, thanks." Hudson declined as well.

His father shrugged. "Well, then. Shall we go straight into dinner?"

If it meant getting this stiff, formal evening over with, Bri was all for food.

The rest of the night proceeded as she'd expected once meeting the Northfields. There were more courses than she could eat in one sitting served by a man and woman in uniform. Martin didn't ask about Hudson's career or how he was enjoying his new jobs; instead he bragged about the family trading business and deals he had in the works. He pushed for Hudson to give up jobs that barely earned him a living and instead come home, where he belonged, to which Hudson adamantly put his foot down.

There was something sexy about a man who knew what he wanted and refused to bow to anyone in order to achieve his goals, but this conversation told Bri how difficult the request for investment money was going to be for Hudson. A talk he planned to have on Sunday morning before they flew home later that afternoon.

Nobody asked Bri what she did for a living, nor did they seem interested in her at all, so she ate in silence and grew angry on Hudson's behalf.

When they were blessedly on dessert and coffee and leaving for the hotel was finally in sight, Lucille spoke up for what seemed like the first time.

"Hudson, darling, I mentioned to Corinne that you would be in town this weekend, and she's hoping you'll give her a call. Find time to get together?" She glanced at Bri. "Hudson and Corinne go way back," she explained, daintily patting her lips with a napkin.

At least Bri hadn't taken a sip of coffee or a bite of pie, because her mouth opened wide. His mother was actually matchmaking while he sat at the table with another woman by his side.

"You know, I assumed since I was bringing a date, you'd have enough class not to mention this ridiculous request again. Apparently I gave you too much credit."

"Hudson!" his father said in a warning tone.

Ignoring him, Hudson yanked the napkin off his lap and tossed it onto the table. "Bri is sitting right here, and you're being rude." He rose from his seat, taking her hand and helping her to her feet.

She managed to lean down, grasp her purse, then take her shawl off the back of her chair.

"For the record," Hudson said, "Corinne and I do not go way back. We aren't even friends. You just keep giving the woman false hope that she can marry into this family, and you need to stop. Now."

"But ... Hudson, don't leave. I won't bring her up again. I just thought..."

"You thought you'd try and run my life in your own way, just like Dad is trying to do in his." Anger vibrated through him, and Bri felt his fury.

She reached for his hand, but her touch did nothing to calm him.

Martin rose from his seat. "Sit down, son."

Hudson shook his head. "I put up with you both pushing me. I'm used to it, but Brianne is my guest, and I won't have her dismissed the way you did tonight. We're leaving, and we'll see you at the wedding." He eased out her chair and guided her toward the arched entry and exit.

"Umm, thank you for dinner," Bri said as he all but pulled her from the room.

She rushed alongside him, waiting until they reached the front door before she came to a halt. "Hudson, go back and make peace. You need something from your father, and this isn't the way to get it." Softening the man up would have been a better angle.

"Actually it was exactly the right move. My father respects a man who stands up for himself. I'll deal with the clinic funds on Sunday. Right now I want to get the hell out of here."

He pulled open the door, and they stepped outside. Hudson sent a text for the driver, letting him know to pull around to the front of the house because they were ready to go.

On the ride home, she gave him space, allowing him the time to lose his anger and refocus his energy. Meanwhile, Bri went over the evening in her mind. And she couldn't deny how much she appreciated Hudson sticking up for her and refusing to let his parents treat her badly. He'd put up with it for himself because they were his mother and father, but he'd drawn the line when it came to Bri. And that fury on her behalf turned her on.

He wouldn't want to hear it now but later? When they got back to the room, she'd let him in on that secret and show him exactly what his protective behavior meant to her.

Chapter Five

Hudson ground his teeth the entire ride from his parents' house back to the city, surprised he hadn't destroyed his molars by the time they reached the hotel. Clearly sensing his anger, Bri remained quiet during the trip, just as she had on their way there. He felt bad enough his mood had been shit, but she'd been dismissed by his mother, and he'd had enough. He'd dragged her out of there as fast as he could and had taken the time since to get himself under control before he did something stupid. Like turn their first time into a release of his frustration instead of making it about them.

Once they returned to the hotel suite, he kicked off his shoes and tossed his jacket over a chair in the outer room. She'd done the same with her heels, then padded on bare feet to where he stood.

Somehow he had to make things right, but after that dinner disaster, he wasn't sure how. He met her gaze and said the first words that came to him. "Tonight never should have happened, and I'm—"

She cut him off by throwing herself into his arms and sealing her lips against his. Obviously she didn't need an apology, though he'd make sure he gave her one. Later.

Right now he had a beautiful woman in his arms who had made her desire for him clear. He shoved his parents' behavior from his mind and turned his focus to Bri.

He pulled her tight against him and took control of the kiss, his tongue thrusting into her mouth and capturing her moan in his throat. Her hands came to his chest, fingers fumbling with the buttons, and he let out a low growl, then broke the kiss and pulled at the sides, sending buttons flying.

"That was sexy." An approving light lit her eyes. "But if you try to rip off my outfit, we're going to have issues," she said with a laugh. "I paid good money for this pantsuit."

"And it was worth every penny." He shrugged off his shirt, pulling his hand through the buttoned sleeves.

"Look at you. Tanned, muscled, hot." She set her palms on his chest, the bandages still there, but the rest of her hand felt warm on his skin. Leaning forward, she pressed her lips to the patch of skin below his throat, licking his flesh with her tongue.

A full-body shudder took hold, and he couldn't take the teasing. "I want to see you naked."

She turned her back to him and moved her hair to one side, her gaze meeting his. "Unzip me then."

He eased down the zipper, revealing the smooth skin on her back, and ran his finger over the bumps in her spine. She shivered before shimmying the top part down her arms, and then the outfit fell to the floor. She slid her feet out of the pant legs and kicked the pooled material aside before pivoting back toward him.

He consumed her with his gaze, taking in her full breasts, creamy mounds pushed up in a strapless bra, and desire flooded his veins. Reaching behind her, he unhooked the clasps and let the garment go, baring her gorgeous breasts and pausing to look his fill.

He drew a shallow breath before dipping his head and was immediately surrounded by the warm coconut scent he'd begun to associate with Bri. From her hair to her body, she always made him think of sunscreen and the beach. Hot, sexy smells he loved.

With a low growl, he pulled one nipple into his mouth, teasing her with a slight grazing of his teeth and lingering with laps of his tongue. She moaned and pulled his head tighter against her chest, allowing him leeway to switch from one breast to the next. With every biting sting and soothing caress, she tugged at his hair and squirmed in reaction.

As far as he was concerned, he could stay like this forever, tormenting her now sensitive breasts, but his cock had a different opinion. It pulsed insistently against his pants, begging to be set free. She must have read his mind, because her hands went to his waistband, and she unhooked his dress pants. It didn't take long for him to shuck the slacks along with his boxer briefs.

Her gaze settled on his large cock, rigid and ready. She grasped him tight and glided up and down his shaft. The sharp sensations ricocheting through him had him curling his hands into fists at his sides. He let her play, but when her thumb swiped over the leaking cum on the head of his dick, he couldn't handle any more.

Though he briefly debated a hard fuck against the wall, that wasn't what he wanted with Bri. "Come on, gorgeous. We're taking this to bed."

She met his gaze, her eyes already dilated and darkened with arousal. "Lead the way."

Grasping her hand, he led her through the outer room and into the large bedroom in the suite. Without waiting, she slid onto the bed, which had already been turned down by housekeeping, and settled against the many pillows in front of the fabric headboard.

Her tanned skin glittered against the white sheets, and he realized she'd put lotion on after her shower. Lotion that must smell like coconut, he mused, ready to dive in for another taste of her skin.

She spread her legs, giving him a look at her sweet pussy. His cock pulsed, and he grabbed it tight, giving himself a few good pumps before climbing onto the bed beside her, the warmth of her body seeping into his. He leaned down and kissed her, not the hot and eager joining of earlier but more of an acknowledgment of the moment and that they were about to do this. Her lips slid back and forth over his, and soon their bodies were aligned and rocking against each other, his thickened cock aching as it pulsed against her lower belly and her sex.

She moaned and reached between them, gripping his cock in her hand. "I need you inside me."

He wanted the same thing, her warm, wet heat tight around him, but he needed protection first. "Condoms are in the bathroom."

He turned and headed for the bathroom, returning with a strip in his hand.

"Someone's anticipating a busy night." Anticipation lit her eyes as he tossed the condoms onto the bed.

Without waiting for him to join her, she grabbed the strip, ripped off one square, and opened the packet. He climbed onto the mattress, straddling her, and she reached out, gripping his cock in her hand. He gritted his teeth, holding on to his control by a thread as she slid the condom over his straining shaft.

Desire beat heavily inside him, and when he glanced down and saw how wet she was, he nearly lost his mind. He held her gaze, unable to look away as he braced his hands above her shoulders, set his cock at her entrance, and easily slid inside.

Her inner walls clasped him tight, warm heat surrounded him, and in that instant, he knew she was different than any woman he'd been with before. Not a socialite his parents paraded in front of him and not someone without substance and depth. Smart, quick, witty, and her body made for him, Brianne Prescott was the whole package. And he intended to make her his.

Starting by claiming her now. He pulled out and thrust back in deep, causing her to cry out in surprise. She dug her nails into his back and arched her hips as each drive inside her was harder and deeper than the last. Their skin grew slick with sweat, and it didn't take long for his balls to draw up and need to hit him hard, but he refused to come without her.

From the way she ground her sex against his pubic bone, she was close. Needing to speed things up while at the same time not wanting this moment to end, he eased a hand between them and slid his finger over her clit, rubbing the tiny bud with his thumb.

"Jesus, Hudson!" Her hips bucked, and she trembled beneath his hand, and soon she was coming, her slick inner walls clasping him tight, bringing him higher.

Her nails scored his back, and he knew he'd have marks, not that he cared. Just then, a strong wave hit him, and he drove into her hard, over and over, pressing her against the bed as he emptied himself in a climax that seemed to go on forever.

He collapsed on top of her with the feeling that something inside him had shifted, and there was no going back to who he'd been. A guy satisfied on his own with occasional stress relief.

Now he was a man who wanted this one woman by his side.

* * * *

Bri stretched her well-used body, knowing she was going to be sore tomorrow and love every minute of the reminder of her time with Hudson. She watched as he strode to the bathroom, taking in his lean but muscular form and his adorably pale behind. She didn't think he'd appreciate her assessment of his ass, so she kept those feelings to herself.

He rejoined her and lifted the covers so they could both get under them. Snuggling against him, she laid her head on his shoulder and let out a sigh.

"What's wrong?" he asked.

"That was a happy sigh," she explained. She didn't know what it was about Hudson, but she felt comfortable with him, like she could let her guard down and just be herself.

"Good," he said, pulling her tighter against him. "So I have to ask. How is it that some athlete you represent hasn't snatched you up by now?"

Glad they couldn't make eye contact during this conversation, instead she focused on her hand drawing circles on his chest. "Well, because they are athletes, probably. I put up a big DO NOT TOUCH sign. Well, I give out those signals, anyway. I learned my lesson over the years, and my trust level isn't all that high."

"Hmmm." She felt the rumble in his throat vibrate through him. "Would you explain?"

She shrugged. Why not, when she trusted him more than any man she'd ever met? "Let's put it this way. I tried dating athletes since that's who I gravitated to and met through my family, but it turned out most men went out with me as a means to an end. They wanted an in with Austin, the agent, or Damon and Jaxon, the athletes."

"Assholes," Hudson muttered.

She grinned. "I appreciate your outrage on my behalf." She drew in a deep breath and let it out before continuing. "So then I tried dating a regular guy. I met him at the coffee shop near the office. He paid for my coffee; we shared a table and hit it off. I figured I was dating a salesman who didn't want anything to do with sports."

"And?" He tangled his fingers in her hair, tugging on the strands as he twisted the long pieces.

"He turned out to sell energy drinks and wanted Damon to endorse the company's newest product. Austin, as Damon's agent, had already turned him down, but he figured I'd have more of an in, being his sister and his publicist. At that point, I pretty much swore off men."

"You deserve someone who wants you for you. For all the special qualities that you bring to the table." His voice came out like a low rumble, and the gruff sound turned her on despite the fact that she'd just come harder than she ever had in her life.

"Care to name those qualities?" she asked, teasing him.

"Are you searching for a compliment?" He pulled her on top of him, and their bodies aligned, his soft cock beginning to harden against her stomach.

She let out a soft laugh. "What woman wouldn't want to hear all her positive traits?"

"Hmm. Well, you're beautiful and intelligent."

Heat rose to her cheeks at the compliments. "Do go on."

He wrapped his hands around her lower back, his fingers resting on her rear end. "You're sexy, you have a great sense of humor, and you know your worth. All things I admire about you."

Her heart softened at his words, and she knew she was falling hard and fast for Hudson Northfield. "And you're the first person to see past my family. The only guy who is with me for me. You don't want or need anything from me, and I appreciate that more than you know."

Her lips slid over his, and soon he was back in charge, giving her deep, drugging kisses that had her head spinning and her body tingling with arousal. He pushed himself off her and ripped a condom from the strip he'd tossed on the bed, tore into it, and rolled it over his now hard cock.

Next thing she knew, he'd sat up and grabbed her around the waist, positioning her over him so his straining cock poised at her entrance. His hands gripped her hips as she lowered herself onto him, and his thick erection stretched her in the best possible way. She closed her eyes and moaned, rocking her body forward and back, waves of arousal lifting her higher.

Her nipples puckered, and he noticed, reaching out and tweaking the hardened tips with his fingers, causing her to clamp around him.

"Fuck. You feel so good."

"So do you." She rode him hard, but no matter what she did, her orgasm remained elusively out of reach. She raised herself up and down, but she couldn't come. "I'm trying, but I can't–" She groaned her frustration.

His dilated gaze softened, and an understanding look crossed his face. "Climb off."

Confused, she settled on her knees beside him. "What's wrong?"

He treated her to a sexy grin. "Not a thing except we're changing positions."

She lifted her eyebrows. "We are?"

He hooked an arm around her waist and whispered in her ear, "Get on all fours, sweetheart. I know how to make you come."

She shivered and did as he asked, settling on her hands and knees. He came up behind her, his hot body covering hers, his thick cock at her entrance. He pushed in, going slow until he filled her, and she sucked in a breath as he bottomed out completely.

After pulling out, he thrust back in, hitting exactly the right spot.

"Yes," she said on a hiss, pushing back against him, and he began repeating the motion. He was right; she would definitely come this way and fast.

Especially when he reached around and slid his finger over her clit. A loud moan escaped her lips, and she trembled. "Harder," she urged him.

Not only did he pick up the pace of each thrust, he rubbed her clit harder, pinching then gliding the pad of a finger over the now sensitive bud. She moaned, bracing her arms for every slam of his body into hers. Feeling him everywhere, she gave herself over to him, allowing him to guide and control both the pace and the timing of when she'd come. She trusted him to take care of her, and he was doing exactly that.

"Turn your head toward me," he said in a rough voice.

She twisted her neck, and he captured her lips in a harsh kiss, all the while grinding his hips against her. His cock hit a place that shattered what little sanity remained.

Their mouths separated as her orgasm began and continued with every push and grind of their bodies together. White stars flashed behind her eyes as a rush sounded in her ears, her entire being alight with pleasure. The gratification continued, a second orgasm coming on the heels of the first at the same time Hudson shouted from behind her. Faster thrusts, another heavy groan, and he stilled, his cock pulsing inside her as he emptied himself, and his climax eased.

They collapsed together on the bed, his hard, sweaty body on top of hers. Her breath came in short pants, and she tried to take slower, steadier streams of air.

He slid out of her, and she felt the loss, the disconnection of their bodies as he rolled to the side. As he propped himself on one arm, his heavy-lidded gaze met hers. "Told you I had it handled."

She grinned, unable to deny he had, in fact, made her come just as he'd promised. "We click," she said, not embarrassed to admit that fact.

"Yes, we do." He kissed the tip of her nose and flipped over, climbing out of bed and walking to the bathroom to dispose of the condom.

He returned and shut off the lights over the bed, joining her under the covers and pulling her tight against him. "I wish we could skip the rest of the family part of the weekend," he muttered.

"It will be fine. I can handle your parents, and I don't take it personally. Ignore them, and we'll have fun. I'm looking forward to meeting Serena. If you two are close, I'm sure I'll like her."

"You will, and she'll like you." He hugged her tighter. "Then I'll get the conversation about funding the clinic over with, and we can head home."

"Sounds good." Her eyelids were getting heavy. "We'll figure everything out," she assured him.

"I believe we can."

* * * *

Serena married in a typical Northfield affair at the country club her parents belonged to. Her now-husband might not be of the same social class, and Serena's parents didn't really approve of the union, but they'd caved and had thrown their only daughter the wedding of her dreams.

Hudson was happy for his cousin, who beamed as he and Bri greeted her on the reception line.

"I've missed you!" Serena pulled him into a big hug, so unlike the older generation of their families who'd air-kissed or shaken hands in greeting.

He wrapped her in an embrace before stepping back so he and his cousin could make the introductions between Bri and Serena's husband, Mark.

When those were complete, Serena looked from Hudson to Bri

and smiled. "I like her, and you look happy," she said as Bri made conversation with Mark.

He had no doubt it was obvious from the way he'd wrapped an arm possessively around her waist that Bri wasn't just arm candy. "That's because I am."

She lifted herself onto her toes and whispered in his ear, "Then don't let her go."

"I don't intend to," he said with a grin.

Beside him, Bri had overheard and turned her head to meet his gaze, eyes wide as he nudged her with his hip. "We should get going and let other people talk to the bride and groom." He winked at her before glancing at the happy couple. "Congratulations and enjoy your lives."

"In other words, ignore the parents. Got it." Serena treated them to a genuine smile. "We will."

"Nice to meet you and congratulations," Bri said, then Hudson led her away from the receiving line, and they made their way to a private corner of the room.

"It was a beautiful ceremony," she said.

He smiled, his eyes on her. "*You're* beautiful."

"You like the dress?" She spun around, giving him a complete view of the rose-gold with lace, low-cut V-neck that accentuated her full breasts and hugged her curves. The choice was the perfect gown for the occasion. And for her body.

Because she'd co-opted their hotel suite for the day for hair, makeup, and who knows what other feminine things, he'd only had a few minutes to change into his tux and get a good glimpse of her fully made-up and dressed before they had to leave. He studied her now, her beautiful face, her unique-colored eyes accentuated with liner and thick lashes, glowing skin, and pink, shiny lips. And her gorgeous dark hair flowed over her shoulders in waves.

"I love everything about you," he said, the words escaping before he could censor them. Taken in context, they could mean anything, but in his heart, they held deeper meaning. He was falling fast for his best friend's sister.

Her eyes opened wide, and her mouth parted in surprise. "I–"

"Son! It's good to see you." His father's voice interrupted them. So typical, as if last night's scene had never happened. At least that boded well for Hudson's money pitch. But his father had shitty timing.

He and Bri turned to face his parents.

"Hello, Mr. and Mrs. Northfield," Bri said with a smile.

They murmured polite hellos back but didn't ask her to be less formal. Also typical.

"Mom, Dad, we were just going to dance." He slid his hand into Bri's. She'd removed her bandages, and the wounds were already beginning to heal.

"You'll come by early tomorrow to talk as planned?" his father asked, an anticipatory and excited gleam in his eyes.

Hudson knew better than to give his father warning about the topic of conversation. Surprise would be on his side. "Yes, I'll be there." And this time, he'd be leaving Bri at the hotel. No need to subject her to his parents' version of politeness, which actually bordered on rude behavior.

"Looking forward to seeing you, son."

His mother patted his shoulder, and they walked away.

"Are they always so pleasant?"

"Unfortunately, yes. There's a reason I'm living in Florida. Can we not focus on them?" he asked, wrapping an arm around her and leading her toward the dance floor.

The rest of the evening passed in a blur of wedding routines, from toasts to someone clinking or tapping glasses together and demanding the bride and groom kiss to the throwing of the garter and the bouquet.

Apparently he and Bri had the same feelings about the rituals, because he'd tried to avoid the cluster of single men grouped to see who caught the item and would be next to marry. As the superstition said. But Serena caught his gaze, walked over, and pulled him into the crowd, positioning him at the right side of the men.

He stood there, feeling like an ass, hating the spectacle, and he wasn't surprised when the groom threw the garter directly to the side Serena had placed him on.

He walked off the dance floor, cheeks burning, garter in his hand, and everyone cheering. Especially Bri, who'd found the entire incident amusing … until Serena pulled the same routine before she tossed the bouquet.

They climbed into the back of the town car Hudson had hired to drive them to and from the hotel, Bri still laughing over their predicaments. "I suppose we're getting married sometime next year," she said, still giggling, slightly tipsy from too much champagne.

He leaned his head back and laughed. "If Serena has her way, we are." He ought to be shaken up by the idea.

He'd never thought about marriage, mostly because any time the subject came up, it had been with his parents after they'd chosen the perfect potential bride. The thought made him want to puke. But the notion of marriage with the right woman, with the woman by his side? That didn't disturb him at all.

But until he had his life settled and knew he had his goals and plans in the works, he couldn't think about the future. In the meantime, he had Bri in his life, and she wasn't going anywhere.

Chapter Six

Bri awoke alone in the large hotel bed Sunday morning. Hudson had gone to meet with his father, and he obviously hadn't disturbed her. Given how late they'd stayed up last night indulging in unrivaled passion, she appreciated him letting her sleep in. Her body was sore from the number of times they'd had sex, using up all the condoms he'd brought with him to New York. She would always remember this weekend as theirs, and she'd had the best time.

After a quick shower, she pulled her hair into a bun and, wearing a hotel robe, stepped into the main area of the suite to find coffee waiting for her along with a basket of muffins.

Her cell rang just as she sat down with her caffeine and blueberry muffin. Macy's name flashed on the screen, and Bri took the call. "Hey!"

"Hey yourself! So how's your weekend going?" Macy asked.

Bri felt her smile grow wide. "Amazing. I mean, Hudson is everything I could want in a man."

"Oh, Bri, I'm so happy for you!" Macy exclaimed loudly.

"He'd better be keeping his hands to himself," Bri's brother Jaxon spoke up in the background.

"Sorry. I should have been quieter," Macy muttered. "Go away," she said to her husband. "This is none of your business." A few seconds passed and she uttered, "Go!" again.

Bri laughed. "If I wasn't used to my brothers and if I didn't know they meant well, I might murder them."

Macy chuckled, too. "Did I interrupt anything?"

"No. Braden has a meeting with his father this morning, so I stayed back at the hotel." Bri took a long sip of her coffee and all but moaned, she needed the caffeine so badly.

"That sounds so formal."

"You should meet these people. They're the epitome of wealth and utter disdain for anyone they find below them in social status. And they're still trying to fix Hudson up with someone suitable." She rolled her eyes at that, because she'd seen Hudson stand up to his parents. For her.

The thought warmed her all over again.

"Were they rude to you?" Macy's outrage sounded over the phone.

"If they were rude to my baby sister, I'm going to kick some ass!" Jaxon said.

Bri rolled her eyes. "Remind him I'm older than him, will you?"

"Be quiet!" Macy yelled, then a muffled sound reached Bri's ears.

"Eew. Tell him not to kiss you while we're on the phone!" Bri wrinkled her nose at the thought of hearing or seeing anything about her brother's sex life.

Macy giggled, and Jaxon muttered something before saying louder, "Love you, Bri!"

"Tell him I love him, too."

"And I love hearing you so light and happy. It sounds like Hudson is good for you," Macy said.

Putting her coffee cup on the table in front of the sofa, she curled her legs beneath her and sighed. "He is. We have a lot in common, and we like each other without conditions or strings. He doesn't need or want anything from me, and that's not just refreshing, it's what I've been looking for in a man." And she'd fallen hard for him. Faster than she'd let her guard down with anyone before.

"Well, when you get back, let's have lunch or coffee and you can tell me more. I have to go help Emma with something, so we'll talk soon?" Macy asked.

"Sounds good. Thanks for checking in. Bye." Bri disconnected the call and settled in to finish breakfast.

She needed to shower and be ready to go when Hudson returned from talking to his father. And she couldn't wait to hear the end result. She prayed he got access to his trust fund so he and Braden could move forward with their plan for the health center they envisioned.

* * * *

Hudson stood in the doorway of his father's study, apprehension filling his veins. He hated to have to ask the man for anything. This was Hudson's money, and he shouldn't have to fight that hard for something that belonged to him. He wished his grandfather had lived long enough to see how different Hudson and his father were, but Gerald Northfield had died when Hudson was young, the trust had been set up for all the grandchildren for tax purposes, and his choice of trustee had made sense at the time.

Hudson's father sat at his desk, head bent as he looked over some papers. Hudson cleared his throat, and Martin raised his head.

Catching sight of him, Martin removed his reading glasses and rose to his feet. "Good morning. I trust you had fun at the wedding?"

Hudson stepped inside and shut the door, not wanting any interruptions. "We did. I'm happy for Serena."

"Yes, well, her choice of grooms leaves something to be desired," Martin said as he stepped around and gestured to the two Queen Anne chairs in front of the mahogany desk.

Since this wasn't the best time to argue, Hudson let the derogatory comment stand, as much as it galled him to do so.

They each took a seat, his father crossing one leg on top of the other. "So. You wanted to talk?"

"I do."

"I admit I'm hoping you've changed your mind about staying in Florida and playing doctor when there's a lucrative business that needs to be run here and its future to be considered."

Hudson drew a deep breath and again ignored the comment he didn't want to address. The last thing he needed to do was get drawn into a fight and lose his higher ground.

He gripped the armrests of the chair tightly. "Actually, I'm staying in Florida."

"Is this about that girl?" His father's face grew red with anger.

"No. This is about me." He hated the denial but knew it was necessary.

At this point, Bri had everything to do with his choices, but he'd already known his plans for his career prior to spending the weekend with her and falling in love. Had it happened fast? Sure, but he trusted his gut. She was it for him.

"Then why? Your family is in New York. The business is in New York."

Leaning forward in his seat, he appealed to a place inside Martin that Hudson wasn't sure existed. "Look, Dad. I'm happy there. And I'm not playing doctor, I am a doctor, and I'm damned good at it. Not only do I have a great job with the Miami Thunder but I'm volunteering at a health clinic in a neighborhood that is desperately in need of medical care."

"And that's more important than your family legacy?" His father sounded horrified.

"Frankly, yes. The clinic is in a depressed area of the city, and my friend and fellow doctor Braden Prescott and I have a plan to remodel the place, invest in state-of-the-art equipment, and treat people who don't otherwise have access to care."

His father narrowed his gaze. "And you're here because you want access to your trust fund, I presume?"

Hudson nodded. "I do. I think your father would like that his money was going for a good cause."

The deep sigh echoed around the room as his father steepled his fingers together in thought. Tense silence passed, and Hudson did his best not to tap his foot impatiently or otherwise rush Martin's thinking process despite his own nerves being on edge. The sound of a clock ticking added to his stress.

"I'll tell you what. I have a proposition for you. A quid pro quo."

Wary now, Hudson clenched his jaw and indicated his agreement to listen with a curt nod.

A pleased smile lifted his father's lips, and Hudson knew he wasn't going to like the proposal. He steeled himself to hear it, certain his father was going to somehow force him to return home and work the business in exchange for the clinic money. In which case he wouldn't be there to see his dream come to life, but the people he'd come to know would have access to everything they needed. But he was getting ahead of himself, and he forced his heart rate to calm as he waited.

His father straightened his posture as he said, "I'll give you the money for your little health care center if you marry and provide your mother and me with an heir."

That idea hadn't even been on Hudson's radar. "What century is this?" he asked, his tone rising.

"Lower your voice. I don't want your mother running in here and interrupting us. Think about it. Your brother is gone, ruining any chances we have of a grandchild, and your mother is distraught about it. The family name needs to live on, and you're the only one who can make that happen."

Hudson rubbed a hand over his eyes before meeting his father's gaze. "What else?" he asked, certain he hadn't heard everything.

"You're a smart man, son. And if I thought for a moment I could force your hand and get you to come home and take over the business, I would. But I know damned well you'd turn me down no matter the consequences."

His father studied him with a hint of... It couldn't be pride Hudson saw. But he was acknowledging Hudson's dedication to his career.

"You're right. So what is the catch?" As he asked, the answer dawned on him and his entire body stiffened. "I am not marrying Corinne," he said, just as adamant about that as he was about staying in Florida.

His father let out a low chuckle. "I realized that as well."

In other words, in the short time since Hudson had asked for the money, his astute father had sifted through all the possible blackmail options and come up with the only one he knew Hudson might agree to.

"You really are a piece of work," he muttered, his gaze settling on one of the expensive paintings on the wall in the office.

Martin Northfield shrugged. "I didn't keep us where we are in life by being stupid." He set his hands on the armrests and pushed himself up from his seat. "So those are my terms. Let me know what you decide. Have a good flight back to Florida," he said and walked out of the room, leaving Hudson alone with the bomb he'd dropped in his lap.

He rested his head against the back of the chair and groaned. Marriage. The idea itself wasn't the problem. He and Bri had laughed about it enough over the weekend, and she hadn't freaked out at the idea. His gut told him she definitely wanted to get married and have children one day with the right man. A man who wanted to marry her because he loved her and for no other reason.

Not twelve hours ago, she'd been in his arms and uttered the very words that put up a roadblock to him asking her now.

You're the first person to see past my family. The only guy who is with me for me. You don't want or need anything from me, and I appreciate that more than you know.

She wouldn't appreciate it if he asked her to marry him so he could get access to the money to fund the clinic. Not at all.

If he told her what happened here today, she might offer to marry him in order to help him achieve his goal, but then she'd never know that he was marrying her because he loved her.

He did, but even he knew they needed more time to cement their relationship. And he'd never take something as important as knowing she was loved away from her. Which meant she could never know that his father had offered him the money with these strings attached. All he could tell Bri was that his parent had turned him down, and after meeting Martin Northfield, she'd have no trouble believing he could do something that cruel.

Son of a bitch, he thought, pissed at his father for fucking up the best thing in his life and putting him in a position of having to give up the clinic, leaving it to Braden to handle alone. Of course, he could go to the bank and attempt to take out a loan, and he would, but he didn't have enough credit to fund what he needed. Only his trust fund had that kind of money, and it was within his father's discretion to turn him down. Unless he got married and knocked up his wife.

Fucking perfect, he thought in disgust. If and when he had children, he swore he'd never use them, treat them like a commodity, blackmail them, or give them anything less than unconditional love and support.

And the same with the woman he loved.

Chapter Seven

For the next few weeks, Bri lived in a state of bliss in her relationship with Hudson. They saw each other at work, sneaking moments alone in her office when they could, and began alternating sleeping over at his apartment and her house, though recently they'd just begun using her house as their base. He brought things over and left them there. Her bathroom now had his razor and shaving cream, toothbrush, and shampoo. *Who knew a man could be fussy about his hair care*, she mused, enjoying having him in her personal space.

She grinned as she dressed for her mother's birthday party they were attending this afternoon. All had been quiet in her work world, no player crises to handle, but Hudson had gone to the stadium to treat some of the players.

He was doing his best to push forward with clinic plans despite having been turned down by his father, who'd refused to release the principal of the trust fund money. So Hudson was busy making appointments with a bank to apply for a loan, and he and Braden were discussing bringing on investors to make their dream a reality.

She had a plan of her own to help him, but she'd wanted the money she hoped to raise to be a surprise, and she intended to fill him in after they returned from the party at her mother's house.

Hudson walked into the house just as she'd entered the kitchen. He dropped his keys in the dish she left for that purpose near the front door and strode up to her, planting a long, deep kiss on her mouth.

"Mmm," she said as he lifted his head. "Do that again."

"My pleasure." He snaked his arm around her, pulling her close and closing his lips over hers.

The kiss sent tremors of awareness sizzling up her spine. She could get used to this, Hudson coming home to her every day, them living in a real home that they made together. In fact, she wanted a future with him with every fiber of her being.

"I love you," she said, shocked when the words came out of her mouth.

He blinked, his eyes opening wide.

"I... You don't have to say it back. I just... It slipped," she said, her face hot with embarrassment.

He cupped her face in his strong hands. "Did you mean it?" he asked, his voice gruff, his expression vulnerable. Unless she was misreading him, which she didn't think she was.

Swallowing hard, she decided to go with the truth. No pain, no gain, as the athletes who surrounded her liked to say. And Hudson had given her no reason not to have hope.

"I do." Her heart pounded so fast in her chest it hurt.

His features softened, those sexy lips turning up in a smile. "Good because I love you, too." His lips came down hard on hers again, his tongue slipping into her willing mouth as he backed her against the nearest cabinet.

They devoured each other, their kisses hot, their bodies grinding against each other to the point where her panties grew damp enough that she knew either they stopped or they'd end up in bed. Which she wanted desperately, but they didn't have the time.

With regret, she pulled away. "If we keep this up, we'll miss the party."

He frowned but released her, taking a few steps back and catching his breath. "I need to shower and then I'll be ready." His gaze skimmed over her outfit, a pair of fitted black pants and a pink scoop-neck top that tucked into the thick waistband.

"You look great." His eyes darkened as they met her gaze, and he inched closer again.

She held up a hand, stopping him before they ended up with their hands all over each other. Again. "Go shower," she said halfheartedly. Because he'd said he loved her, too, and she really wanted to take the time and enjoy the moment.

"Later," he promised in that deep voice she adored. He jogged out of the kitchen, and a few minutes later, she heard the running of the shower.

Smiling, she stopped in the bathroom and checked her makeup in the mirror. Some gloss and she'd be okay. Then she grabbed her mother's present and slipped on her shoes, waiting for him when he joined her, ready to go.

A little while later, they were at her mom's house along with her entire family. Bri gave her mom the gift she'd picked out, her favorite perfume in a special-edition bottle she could set on her dresser, and she and Hudson separated as they caught up with different people.

Macy and Jaxon had brought Emma, Macy's sister, who, after going through a rough patch, was blossoming living with the newly married couple. To Bri, the teenager already felt like part of her family. While she and Macy spoke, her mom grabbed Emma's hand and dragged her into the kitchen for homemade brownies, and it was obvious Emma basked in the glow of all the mothering she got from Christine. Nothing made Bri's mother happier than taking in a stray and making them feel at home.

Bri spent a few minutes talking with Jaxon and Macy and Willow, who was with them, before moving on to Damon and Evie. "So how's my retired brother?" she asked, nudging him in the ribs.

After a horrible concussion on the field last month, Damon's doctors had looked at his history of head injuries and told him if he continued to play, he'd risk the rest of life as he knew it mentally. Damon hadn't had to think twice. He'd chosen to be around for his family, taking a job with Dare Nation, and was now learning the ropes of being an agent.

"How does it look like I'm doing?" He wrapped an arm around Evie and pulled her close, pressing a kiss to her cheek. "I'm fine."

"How are you?" Evie asked.

Bri smiled. "I'm good! Busy with work but that's nothing new."

"And Hudson? He's treating you well?" Damon asked. "Or do I have to kick his ass?"

Bri rolled her eyes. "Oh my God, you sound like Braden. Stop! He's been amazing."

"Good," Evie said, then glanced at her husband. "And you need to mind your own business."

Bri grinned and shot her sister-in-law an appreciative look. "See? We women stick together. Now I'm going to get a soda. See you later."

She walked into the large state-of-the-art kitchen her mother adored, with the stainless steel, high-end appliances, and custom white

Italian-made cabinets.

Grabbing a can of soda from the Sub-Zero refrigerator and a glass from the cabinet, she added ice and poured her drink before joining Austin and Quinn by the center island. Jenny snuggled against her brother, her big blue eyes on Bri. She held out her arms and, while making bubbles with her mouth, reached for Bri, practically throwing herself forward.

"Come here, my favorite little girl." She settled the baby on her hip and placed a smacking kiss on her chubby cheek. "She smells so good."

"It's the shampoo. Nothing smells better than a freshly washed baby," Quinn said with a grin.

"It's getting her clean that's the challenge. All the water splashing with her hands and feet." Austin looked at his daughter with so much love in his eyes, it was a beautiful thing to see, and when he turned to Quinn, love exploded between them.

Bri's heart squeezed, and for the first time since all of her brothers had found love, she could say the same. Suddenly she missed Hudson and needed to feel his arms around her so she could bask in their earlier admission. She loved him, and he loved her back. Holding back her smile so her smart sibling didn't question why she'd suddenly begun grinning, she handed Jenny back to Quinn and went looking for Hudson.

* * * *

Hudson and Braden huddled in the study while the party went on in other rooms of the house. There was a sofa against one wall where the women left their handbags, and Jenny's diaper bag sat on the floor beside the couch. The study had French doors that remained open, because nothing about this conversation was that private. Although they worked together, neither man wanted to talk about their clinic plans while at another job, so now was as good a time as any.

Braden leaned against the desk in the room while Hudson paced the hardwood floor covered by an area rug.

"The bank wants collateral, which I don't have," Hudson said, picking up the conversation where they'd left off last time they'd had this discussion.

Braden narrowed his gaze. "You know, you never did tell me about the talk you had with your father. Just that he turned you down. But you hinted there was more to the conversation than a flat-out no, so what gives?"

Despite the fact that Hudson was frustrated with his inability to get money from his father, he hadn't told his friend the entire conversation. Not only were the stipulations ridiculous, but he was embarrassed to have such an ass for a parent.

With a groan, Hudson ran a hand over his hair. "You wouldn't believe it if I told you."

Braden folded his arms across his chest and met Hudson's gaze. "Try me. We can't work this out if I don't know everything."

Hudson nodded. "Well, my father didn't outright say no to giving me the money. He just placed some conditions on releasing the funds that I haven't figured a way around."

Eyebrows raised, Braden waited.

Hudson winced as he said, "He'll give me the money if I get married and provide him and my mother an heir."

"You've got to be fucking kidding me. What century is this?" Braden's outrage matched his own.

"That's what I asked, but he's not backing down." In fact, his father had followed up with not one but two phone calls since their visit, asking if Hudson had made up his mind.

Braden straightened and walked over to where Hudson stood. "So how badly do you want the money? Enough to get married and get your wife to pop out a kid?" Braden asked, obviously kidding because he knew Hudson better than that, and besides, Hudson was with Bri. And she didn't deserve to get involved in his father's quid pro quo.

"It wouldn't hurt," Hudson said back, equally joking because there'd never been a moment when he'd considered his father's demands.

"I'm sorry, what?" Bri stood in the doorway, one hand on the molding, staring at them both in disbelief.

Motherfucker. "Bri, that was not what it sounded like."

The color had drained from her face, and she now clutched that molding in a death grip. "Really? Because it *sounded* like you need a wife and a kid to get the money from your father."

She looked from her brother to Hudson, obviously feeling

betrayed, and he understood why. "Bri—"

"Is that why you told me you loved me?" she asked, her lower lip quivering.

"Aww, shit," Braden muttered. "You're taking things out of context."

"I heard it myself." She glared at Hudson. "Well?"

"You said it first," he reminded her, because he wanted her to understand that he hadn't come to her with the words because he wanted something from her. He'd said them back because he meant them.

She stepped away from the doorframe and rested her hands on her hips. "Oh, so I gave you the opening you needed. That's just great! I asked you what your father said, and you told me he turned you down!" Her voice rose, and he winced, not wanting more of an audience than the one they had.

"Because as far as I'm concerned, he did. Look—" Before he could explain further, she brushed past him and stopped at the sofa, grabbing the big purse she always carried. "What are you doing?"

She pulled out a folder and clutched it in her hands. "I was going to show you this tonight, after the party. I've set up a huge fundraiser and invited the biggest names I know to bid on high-end items with the proceeds going to the clinic. And trust me, with offerings like a week at Asher Dare's Bahamas home, you'll have all the money you need. No reason to get married."

She slapped the folder onto the desk. Hard. "I'm assuming you would have gotten around to that question eventually."

Reaching for her, he grasped her arm. "We need to talk. You don't understand."

"I do. You're just another guy in a long line of them who needs something from me. Even if we didn't start out that way, that's where we ended up. I'm never enough." She turned and rushed from the room, leaving him stunned.

"Shit," Braden said. "Go! Talk to her!"

Hudson had almost forgotten he was in the room. "Your sister has a huge heart, and she's generous beyond belief. But I have a feeling there is no way she's going to believe anything I say." He'd seen the set of her jaw, the stubborn look on her face.

While she'd proven to him with more than words that she loved him, she'd overheard the one thing certain to drive her away, costing them any chance at a future.

But he wasn't giving up without a fight, and he bolted after her, coming to a stop in the living room, where half her family stood. "Where's Bri?"

"She came out of the office upset, asked for a set of car keys, and I gave her ours." Macy walked up to him, anger etching her features. "I don't know what you did but fix it," she said, then turned her back on him and walked away.

* * * *

Bri knew she'd escaped in the nick of time before Hudson or her brother came after her. It wasn't in her nature to run, but this was different. Hudson was supposed to have been different. The one man who fell in love with *her*, no strings, nothing she could do for his career or his future, and she'd told him as much. No wonder he hadn't revealed what his father's stipulation for the money had been. It was much easier to guide her into marriage to save his dream, and she'd made it so easy by saying *I love you* first.

When in the world would she learn?

Driving Macy and Jaxon's car, she pulled into her driveway. Someone would give them a ride here to pick up the car later, and she appreciated the fact that her friend hadn't asked any questions. One look at the tears in Bri's eyes had been enough for her to hand them over.

She left the keys under the floor mat for whoever picked up the vehicle, walked into her house, locked her doors, and set the alarm. Too bad she'd given Hudson a key and her code, but hopefully he'd be smarter than to show up here without her okay.

She dragged herself into her bathroom and washed off her makeup, then changed into a pair of shorts and a T-shirt before heading to the kitchen. Because what did any normal woman do after being betrayed? She pulled out her favorite mint chip ice cream, grabbed a spoon, and made her way back to her bed, where she turned the television on to some mindless show and proceeded to down the entire pint.

When her phone began to buzz, she allowed herself to look at the screen. Noting it was Hudson, she powered off her cell. She didn't want to hear what he had to say.

The next morning, she turned on her phone to find he'd blown up it up with calls and texts. Most of her family had done the same. Bitch that she felt like being, she refused to read the messages or listen to the voicemails. Thanks to lack of sleep and maybe some crying, she looked awful. She had circles under her eyes, and her face remained blotchy, so she did what she could with makeup. Which wasn't much because her mood showed in her expression. She'd never been good at hiding her emotions when hurt.

And her heart felt like it had shattered.

Since it was Sunday, she didn't have to go to the office. The Thunder weren't playing until four p.m., and she didn't plan on watching the game in case she caught a quick glimpse of Hudson working on the sidelines. No matter what she put on television, the conversation between Hudson and Braden repeated itself over and over in her head.

"He'll give me the money if I get married and provide him and my mother an heir," Hudson said, stopping Bri cold in the doorway.

"You've got to be fucking kidding me. What century is this?" Her brother had sounded pissed.

"That's what I asked, but he's not backing down."

"So how badly do you want the money? Enough to get married and get your wife to pop out a kid?" Braden asked.

Her twin knew Bri was involved with Hudson, so she had no doubt he'd been joking. But Hudson's next words had devastated her.

"It wouldn't hurt."

It wouldn't hurt for him to get married and pop out a kid, as her brother had so crudely put it, and they all knew who the candidate for the role would be. What she couldn't reconcile was how her brother could have sided with him. He said she'd taken Hudson's words out of context, but what other conclusion should she have drawn?

She pulled out her phone and ordered in more ice cream, enough to fill her freezer, from the supermarket, and spent the day watching comedies that didn't make her laugh.

Around two, her phone rang, and a glance told her it was Austin. She frowned but took the call just in case it was about her family. "Hello?" she asked warily.

"Hey. There's a situation in the locker room with your client Dion Davis. He had a fistfight with an attendant because his towels were still damp and he took a swing. The guy set Dion up because he had a camera going, but it's a problem, and you need to get down here and do damage control. You know how Dion gets when he's pissed off, and with the media involved…"

He trailed off, but Bri was already out of her pity party seat on the couch and pulling on clothes in her bedroom. Not long after, she sat in the office of Ian Dare, owner of the Miami Thunder and also her cousin, along with Austin, Dion's agent. Ian was reading her hair-trigger, prima-donna PR client the riot act. Why a grown man couldn't keep his temper in check for a two-million-dollar paycheck with his contract coming up and an even bigger payday ahead was beyond her.

Finally, they'd calmed the beast, and Dion headed back down to his teammates. She and Austin walked out of the room to find Ian waiting in the hall, suit on, arms folded across his chest.

"Well?"

"He'll calm down," Austin promised.

"And I'll see if I can get the attendant not to press assault charges. After all, he lost his job, and the whole thing was a setup. He's after money he's not going to get. Not when I have his phone with the evidence." Ian patted his jacket pocket.

Bri nodded in thanks. She was used to dealing with people who were after money from her clients, who made false pregnancy claims and generally were after something they didn't deserve.

"Now if you'll both excuse me, I have a game to watch." Ian walked away, turning around long enough to say, "I left word for you both to be let up to my box" before walking away.

She looked up at her brother. "I hadn't planned to watch the game."

Austin's gaze softened. "I don't know what happened exactly but–"

"Can we leave it that way? I don't feel like rehashing it."

He wrapped an arm around her shoulder. "Sure. Let's stay for the game, okay?"

Swallowing hard, she nodded. "Sure. It'll be good to spend time with you that has nothing to do with work."

They headed to Ian's box, a place the entire family had been before, and she watched the game, deliberately keeping her gaze away from the sidelines and Hudson, the man watching out for injuries as he did his job.

She and Austin didn't discuss her private life, for which Bri was grateful. Instead she listened to her brother talk about how Jenny had had a growth spurt and was in the next size baby clothes and other milestones, things that at one time would have sent the man who'd sworn to be a bachelor forever running far and fast. Bri soaked in all the news about her niece because she adored that baby, and the chitchat distracted her from her emotional pain.

Her phone buzzed, and she checked the screen. Someone had obviously told Braden she was here because he'd sent a text asking her to meet him by the locker room after the game.

Since she needed a word with her twin, she stayed after the Thunder won. She and Austin said goodbye, and Bri gathered her bag, heading out of the box and down the stairs, walking to where Braden had said they'd meet.

Leaning against the wall in the dimly lit hallway, she watched as people came and went. A few minutes later, the double doors swung open, and she looked up to see Hudson step out. Her stomach twisted as she glanced at him. Wearing a pair of dark chinos and a black Thunder shirt, he stopped short when he saw her, his eyes opening wide.

Their gazes met and held, and everything she felt for him welled up inside her.

"You haven't returned my calls or texts, and I want to explain," he said gruffly.

Before she could answer, he stepped closer, and she caught sight of his painful-looking black eye. "Oh my God! What happened?" Instinct had her reaching to touch the bruise, but she stopped herself and lowered her arm.

"Your brother," he muttered. "But forget about that."

"Which one?" She needed to know which sibling she'd have to kill. The only one she could exclude was Braden.

Hudson held up his hands. "I plead the Fifth. Anyway, it doesn't matter. I deserved it for not being up-front with you about what my father said."

She ground her teeth but had no plans to argue when he was right.

Not about one of her brothers punching him but about not telling her everything.

"Can we talk?" he asked.

She crossed her arms in front of her chest, needing distance, because all she wanted to do was forget yesterday had happened and go back to when she believed they'd had a future.

A lump rose to her throat, and she had to force out the words on her mind. "I'll admit I don't know what happened or why. And that maybe I jumped to conclusions about something I don't understand … but you lied to me."

"I know, and I'm sorry." He looked down, obviously upset with himself.

She wasn't sure how to reply, so she remained silent.

Hudson ran a hand through his hair and groaned. "Take all the time you need. I'm not going anywhere, and we can talk when you're ready."

"Don't you need a wife? I'd think that would put a rush on whatever happens next."

He winced but lifted his chin and solidly met her gaze. "I'm not marrying anyone for money. I never was."

She opened her mouth to reply when Dion came barreling out of the doors in front of her. "Brianne, tell me I kicked ass today on that field!" he said, pride in himself clear.

"Good job, Dion. Now control that temper," she warned him. He grinned, saluted, and strode off, probably to celebrate because that was who he was.

She was about to address what Hudson had just said when the double doors opened again, and this time Braden strode out.

His gaze shot between them, and he winced, obviously catching on that he'd interrupted something. "Umm, sorry, but do you think this is the best place for a private conversation?"

Hudson shook his head. "We're not talking, at least not yet. No worries. If you need me, I'll be in the office," he told Braden. He glanced at her, his gaze saying what words couldn't before he strode down the hall.

Braden raised his eyebrows at her in clear frustration.

"What?" she asked defensively, though she did feel guilty for not letting Hudson explain. But the memory of all the men before him who had used her for one reason or another stayed with her, and when she'd heard Hudson's words and realized he'd lied, he'd broken something precious between them.

It was easier to focus her anger on her twin, and she took two steps forward, giving him a hard shove. "You're a jerk!"

"Hey, what did I do?"

She frowned at him because to her it was obvious. "You took Hudson's side, and you let Damon, Austin, or Jaxon hit him!"

A smirk lifted Braden's lips, and he shook his head, finally letting a laugh escape. "Pick one, Bri. Either you're mad at him or you're not."

She couldn't help the pout that pursed her lips. "I hate you."

"No you don't. But you're being a stubborn princess, and it's not like you to jump to conclusions at something you overheard or to ignore everyone's calls. We're all worried about you."

"I'm allowed time to process," she said, annoyed he didn't understand her feelings.

"You're not processing. You're sulking."

She tucked a strand of hair that had fallen out of her ponytail behind her ear. "Same thing," she grumbled.

Her brother grasped both her forearms. "Look. I get you're pissed. Hudson should have been up-front with you about what his father wanted in exchange for the money. He wasn't honest with me, either. Not until yesterday but I think he was humiliated. It's embarrassing to have to ask for money and get forced into a corner."

She knew that. She'd just been so shocked and hurt, the words she'd heard throwing her back to other times, other men.

"You need to listen to what he has to say," Braden said. "And you also need to decide if you really think Hudson is like the guys who came before him or if he's different and deserves you. I happen to think he does."

And that was saying something, Bri knew. Her twin never approved of anyone she dated. Nobody was ever good enough.

"Who hit him?" she asked, ignoring his words for now. She'd deal with her life and with Hudson on her own terms.

As if they'd planned it, Braden held his hands up just as Hudson had. "You won't hear who from me."

"Men!" she shouted at him just as a group of players exited the locker room, laughing and rowdy, drowning out her yell.

Chapter Eight

Bri hated being stubborn, but she meant what she'd told Braden. She needed time to process what had happened, and that took her a couple more days. First she'd had to separate her past from her present, and that wasn't easy. It meant she had to remember the assholes who'd used her, and there hadn't been just one.

Then she'd had to deal with the fact that Hudson hadn't trusted her enough to tell her the truth when all she'd done was stand by his side. She'd gone to New York, subjected herself to his rude parents, waited at the hotel while he went to ask his father for the money, and held his hand during his brooding silence on the flight home. He'd had a few weeks since then to open up, and he hadn't. Trust was important, but was it a deal breaker?

She supposed that depended on his reasons, and she hadn't let him explain. Which brought her to now, looking at herself in the mirror and admitting she'd been exactly what her brother called her. A stubborn princess and it was time she acted like an adult.

After stopping at a sandwich shop on the way to the clinic, she drove downtown and pulled into the gravel parking lot. Her hands had healed, and she wasn't surprised when she saw Jimmy standing by a dumpster in the back of the lot. She drew a deep breath and climbed out of her car, food in hand, not surprised when Jimmy walked toward her.

"Hi," she said, holding out the sandwich she'd brought him.

"Is that for me?" Surprise filled his gritty voice.

She nodded. "There's water in there, too." And also a twenty-dollar bill, but since she didn't want a repeat of last time, she didn't mention the money. He'd find it soon enough.

He grabbed the bag, and this time she released her grip fast so he didn't drag her down. It helped that she was wearing sneakers and not heels.

"Take care, Jimmy." She walked toward the building, in her mind already thinking about all the improvements Hudson and her brother could make once they were ready and excited about the prospect.

She let herself in, discovered a full waiting room, and resigned herself to wait. Striding up to the desk, she smiled at Nikki. "Hi. Do you think I could wait in the back office until Hudson has time to talk?"

The brunette smiled. "Sure. Dr. Northfield is the only one here, so it may be awhile."

"That's fine." After the torture she'd probably put him through, she deserved to be kept waiting.

Bri made herself at home in the office Hudson and Braden shared, smiling at the pictures on the desk of her twin and Willow, whose wedding was coming up in a few months. May fifth to be exact. They planned a small affair at a local catering hall because July in Florida was just too hot to hold an outdoor event.

An hour passed and then another. The longer she waited, the more her nerves increased. Did Hudson not want to see her, or was he just so busy he couldn't make time yet? Her stomach knotted, and she tried to kill time scrolling social media on her phone and occasionally attempting to read a book on an app, but she couldn't concentrate. She was afraid she'd pushed him too far by not talking to him after the game, but then she reminded herself of the filled outer room and tried to calm down.

After a while, she rested her head on her arms on the desk and shut her eyes.

* * * *

What a fucking long day. Hudson had back-to-back patients, each one serious in its own way, and with Braden needing the day off and Thomas having abdicated the place to Braden and Hudson, he'd been on his own. Thank God for Janie, the nurse they'd recently hired, who was as reliable as she was efficient. Even Nikki had abandoned them midday when her mother called because she'd had an accident, and Nikki had to rush off to be with her. He hadn't had five minutes to eat, let alone sit down and take a load off his feet.

He opened the door to his office and stopped short at the sight that greeted him. Bri sat in his chair, head resting on her arms on the desk, her dark hair falling over her shoulders and face. Even so, he knew it was her, and his heart started beating again for the first time since his fuckup at her mother's house.

He supposed that Nikki, in the frenzied worry about her mother, had forgotten to tell him Bri was waiting, and he wondered how long she'd been here.

He unhooked his stethoscope and laid it on a filing cabinet and took off the white medical jacket he'd taken to wearing here before walking over and placing his hand on her back.

"Bri?" She didn't move, so he rubbed her shirt with his hand. "Hey, beautiful, wake up."

"What?" Startled, she jumped in her seat, her entire body jerking upright, twisting her head up to meet his gaze. "Hudson! Jesus, you scared me. I must've fallen into a really deep sleep."

"Apparently," he said with a chuckle. "How long have you been here?"

She blinked and glanced at her watch. "Three hours. Nikki didn't tell you I was here?"

He shook his head. "Her mom had an accident, and she rushed out. Sorry about that. But it was an insane day. I just locked the place up before coming in here."

"It's fine. I didn't mind waiting." Now that the fright had passed, she looked wary of him, and he didn't like the feeling.

He pulled Braden's chair over and settled in beside her.

"Your eye looks better." Obviously she wasn't ready to jump into the heavy conversation.

"It's fading to a nice shade of puke yellow." Damon had a mean punch, but Hudson refused to out which brother had hit him.

All three had seen their sister crying, and Damon had gotten to him first. It had taken Braden and his shrill whistle to calm everyone down and tell them it was a misunderstanding and none of their business. Then Christine Prescott had issued a stern warning to her sons, but the joy of the day was gone.

Hudson had driven Macy and Jaxon to Bri's house to get her car, and Jaxon had remained there, watching, until Hudson had gotten into his car and gone home. By then he'd already texted Bri a few times and called twice. He'd figured out she wasn't ready to talk to him, so leaving was his best option. He owed her mother a happier birthday party and Bri a lot more.

Bri reached out, and this time, she allowed herself to touch him, gently palpating around his eye. "Does it hurt?"

"Nah. I'm fine."

She rolled her eyes. "Of course you are. Far be it from a man to admit weakness."

He took her soft hand in his. "*You're* my weakness, and I'm not ashamed to admit it."

She glanced down at their hands, and he did, too, noticing how much more tanned and rough his skin was than hers.

"I'm so used to expecting the worst from men, I overreacted. I heard something, and I jumped to the worst possible conclusion, but that would never have happened if you'd just told me the truth."

"You're right. But you have to understand my position. You'd just admitted to me that I was the first guy not to want something from you. I knew how you felt about it, and there was no way I'd ever put you in a position where you didn't know if I was asking you to marry me for money or because I loved you." Just the thought made him physically sick.

"And if I told you what my asshole father wanted, you'd probably have offered to marry me so I could get the clinic money, and then you'd always wonder and be insecure." He waited until she lifted her head and met his gaze. "And I'd never do that to you."

Her eyes filled with tears. "I should have stayed and heard you out, but your words were so damning, and on top of saying you loved me just an hour or so before? I thought for sure I'd fallen into the same trap all over again."

"I made the wrong choice, and though we all know I'll make more mistakes in the future, I promise you'll never doubt that I love you again. Do you forgive me?"

She nodded, a smile on her beautiful face. "Do you forgive me for stringing this out and making you wait?"

He grinned. "I'd wait forever for you, and don't you forget it."

"I can promise you I won't."

They each leaned forward, their mouths meeting in a long kiss that ended too soon.

"Now about that fundraiser." She'd left the folder in his possession when she'd run from the house, and in the days that had passed, he'd been through it over and over. "I cannot believe what you put together in such a short time. The items the guests will bid on will go for thousands each."

A trip to the Bahamas on Asher Dare's private plane and a week in his beach house, front-row seats to concerts and sporting events, a visit to a movie set, and more.

He couldn't begin to name them all or imagine how much money the event would raise. "You did all that for me?"

She nodded. "Because I love you."

"So you'll be my date for the event?" he asked.

"You know I will."

Satisfied, he held her hands tighter. "Just so we're clear, you're mine, Bri. And I love you for the amazing, wonderful woman that you are."

Her answering smile hit him in the heart.

"I know," she said, a saucy glint in her eyes. "You love me enough to take a punch from my brothers and not tell me which one hit you." She shook her head and laughed. "I'd call that true love."

"You're damned right," he said and sealed his lips over hers.

Epilogue

The night of the fundraiser, Hudson found himself in his tuxedo, watching while Bri worked the room like the pro she was. He didn't know whether to be more proud or grateful that she'd put her talents to use to make his dream come true. He didn't deserve her, but he wasn't letting her go.

Sliding his hand into his front pants pocket, he touched the ring he'd gotten from his grandmother when he'd turned twenty-one. His parents might be assholes, but his grandparents had been the best, and his grandmother had wanted him to give her ring to the woman he loved. It had sat in a safe deposit box for years. Until Bri.

The elegant ballroom she'd talked Nick Dare, the entrepreneur Dare and her cousin on her biological father Paul's side, into donating his Miami hotel ballroom for the event. The space was filled with the Who's Who of Miami and other parts of the country, athletes Bri represented, actors and rock stars who were somehow related to the Dare family, and friends and colleagues of theirs. The list went on of people all willing to shell out big money for large-ticket items and who had already paid a hefty per-plate fee.

She glided around the room in her cobalt-blue dress—he knew this after making the mistake of calling it navy blue—making effortless conversation with everyone invited, thanking them for their generosity. Every once in a while, he caught up with her and pulled her into the hallway for a few moments alone.

Like now.

He needed a minute with her before he made a spectacle of

himself in front of the famous people in this crowd. Since the men who had her attention were her siblings, he hooked an arm around her waist.

"Gentlemen, I'm stealing your sister for a few minutes." Hudson had already asked their permission to marry her – more like he'd told them he intended to do so — seeing as how they were the males in her life, and he didn't want another black eye by springing the news on them in front of a crowd.

Without waiting for a reply, he pulled her away from her family and led her out the ballroom doors, finding a corner in the front of the event hall and backing her against a wall.

"Have I thanked you yet?" he asked, his hands on her hips.

She treated him to a radiant smile. "Only a half dozen times. You don't need to thank me. We do things for people we love."

She linked her arms around his neck and rubbed her body against him, making him wish he could kiss that red lipstick off her lips, hike up her dress, and bury himself inside her, but he'd have to put that off until they were alone tonight.

"I love you, too. You have no idea how much." His voice sounded gruff to his ears.

At his pronouncement, her eyes glittered with happiness.

A state of being he'd become familiar with since she'd managed to put his fuckup behind him and everything had been picture-perfect between them since.

"The good news is we are going to net enough money from this event, added with Braden's, for you both to begin renovations on the clinic and purchase new equipment."

"This is everything. I didn't know I had a need to give back until Doctors Without Borders and then working at that run-down clinic. But it fills a need deep inside me. And so do you."

The ring felt heavy in his pocket, which was ridiculous, but the knowledge of what he was about to do had him worked up, and he glanced at his watch. "We need to get back to the ballroom. I have an announcement to make."

She narrowed her gaze. "What kind of an announcement?"

"A surprise one. Now let's go." Hand in hand, they strode back into the ballroom.

* * * *

Bri walked with Hudson as he led them to the front near the deejay and emcee hired for the night. Within a few seconds, the music came to a stop, which caused confused murmurs around the room.

"As you all know, we are here to raise money for a worthy cause. The Prescott Northfield Health Clinic," the emcee began, and the crowd clapped in approval. "You've all had an opportunity to place your bids on the items laid out in our smaller room next to this one."

Bri had been through this with the party planner she'd hired and had walked the room earlier tonight. Some items, such as signed football jerseys, helmets, baseballs, and the like, were visible in a protective case, while things like vacations were listed on a propped sign so people could look over their options and decide what they wanted to bid on. There were also printed brochures on each seat at tables of ten.

The emcee continued his explanation. "You've been assigned paddles, and bidding will begin at ten p.m. Now, before I let you return to your evening and the delicious meal to follow, Hudson Northfield would like to say a few words."

As Hudson made his way to the podium, Bri clapped along with the rest of the guests, surprised when her family surrounded her. She glanced around her to see her mother and a man she'd just started dating along with her brothers and all of their wives.

She'd known they were in attendance, but why were they crowding her now? "What's going on?" she asked.

Before anyone answered her, Hudson began to speak. "Welcome, everyone, and thank you for joining us tonight. Braden and I appreciate the generosity you've shown for a project that is very close to our hearts. There's nothing better in life than giving back and helping others. You are all enabling us to do that, and you have our eternal gratitude."

During the clapping that followed, Bri turned to her twin. "I can't believe you let him have the spotlight all to himself."

He shook his head and grinned. "Shhh," he said, and she pivoted back to face the stage.

She looked up at Hudson, so handsome in his tuxedo. He took her breath away, and he was all hers. She'd learned a hard lesson about listening in, jumping to conclusions, and not trusting her heart.

"Tonight wouldn't have been possible without one person," he said, and her face began to heat because she knew he was referring to her. "You all know her because she's probably called you, badgered you, begged, and pleaded to pull this fundraiser together in a short time. Brianne, would you join me?" He extended his arm and gestured for her to come.

Amidst the clapping, she walked to the three steps leading up to the makeshift podium, lifting her dress as she made her way to Braden. She was used to behind-the-scenes work, and being the center of attention wasn't her thing, but she smiled at the applause.

"Okay, so now for the big event of the evening, at least for me," Hudson said.

Bri heard ripples of laughter, but she wasn't sure where they were coming from or what was going on.

His gaze on hers, his expression completely open, love in his eyes, he said, "Sometimes in life, the unexpected happens, and you meet someone who completes you."

He took her hand in his, and her heart began to pound rapidly in her chest. Why, she didn't know, but she had the sense something monumental was about to happen and swallowed hard.

"You're lucky in that you know what family means and how important it is to have in your life. I didn't know what that was like until I met you."

When he slipped his other hand, the one not holding hers, into his pocket, she began to tremble, and when he pulled out a solitaire diamond ring, her eyes opened wide.

Then he dropped down on one knee. "Brianne Prescott, will you marry me and officially become my family?"

"Say yes!" someone shouted from the crowd.

Laughing, smiling, and crying at the same time, she nodded. "Yes. Yes! I'll marry you."

More applause sounded around them as he slipped the ring on her finger and rose to his feet. Next thing she knew, he'd pulled her into his arms and his lips came down hard on hers. She might have given him a family, but in him she'd found home.

* * * *

Also from 1001 Dark Nights and Carly Phillips, discover Sexy Love, Take the Bride, and His to Protect.

Sign up for the 1001 Dark Nights Newsletter
and be entered to win a Tiffany Key necklace.

There's a contest every month!

Go to www.1001DarkNights.com to subscribe.

As a bonus, all subscribers can download
FIVE FREE exclusive books!

Discover 1001 Dark Nights Collection Eight

Go to www.1001DarkNights.com for more information.

DRAGON REVEALED by Donna Grant
A Dragon Kings Novella

CAPTURED IN INK by Carrie Ann Ryan
A Montgomery Ink: Boulder Novella

SECURING JANE by Susan Stoker
A SEAL of Protection: Legacy Series Novella

WILD WIND by Kristen Ashley
A Chaos Novella

DARE TO TEASE by Carly Phillips
A Dare Nation Novella

VAMPIRE by Rebecca Zanetti
A Dark Protectors/Rebels Novella

MAFIA KING by Rachel Van Dyken
A Mafia Royals Novella

THE GRAVEDIGGER'S SON by Darynda Jones
A Charley Davidson Novella

FINALE by Skye Warren
A North Security Novella

MEMORIES OF YOU by J. Kenner
A Stark Securities Novella

SLAYED BY DARKNESS by Alexandra Ivy
A Guardians of Eternity Novella

TREASURED by Lexi Blake
A Masters and Mercenaries Novella

THE DAREDEVIL by Dylan Allen
A Rivers Wilde Novella

BOND OF DESTINY by Larissa Ione
A Demonica Novella

THE CLOSE-UP by Kennedy Ryan
A Hollywood Renaissance Novella

MORE THAN POSSESS YOU by Shayla Black
A More Than Words Novella

HAUNTED HOUSE by Heather Graham
A Krewe of Hunters Novella

MAN FOR ME by Laurelin Paige
A Man In Charge Novella

THE RHYTHM METHOD by Kylie Scott
A Stage Dive Novella

JONAH BENNETT by Tijan
A Bennett Mafia Novella

CHANGE WITH ME by Kristen Proby
A With Me In Seattle Novella

THE DARKEST DESTINY by Gena Showalter
A Lords of the Underworld Novella

Also from Blue Box Press

THE LAST TIARA by M.J. Rose

THE CROWN OF GILDED BONES by Jennifer L. Armentrout
A Blood and Ash Novel

THE MISSING SISTER by Lucinda Riley

Discover More Carly Phillips

Sexy Love: A Sexy Series Novella

Learning curves have never been so off-limits.

Professor Shane Warden is on the verge of getting tenure. He never thought he'd see the day, after a false accusation from a student years ago that nearly destroyed his career, and decimated his ability to trust. But the moment he walks into class and lays eyes on the seductive blonde with legs that go on forever and lips he immediately wants to kiss, he knows he's in trouble.

This time for real.

Single mom Amber Davis is finally living her dream of going back to college. In the ten years since she dropped out to have a baby--and recover from his father's death--it's been the goal that always felt just out of reach. Until now. But one look at her hot, sexy professor, and Amber is head over heels in lust. It doesn't take long before their attraction blazes out of control.

Neither of them can afford a forbidden affair.

Yet it's the one thing they are powerless to stop.

It will only take one hint of a rumor to destroy everything they've worked so hard to achieve... and in this case the rumors are true.

* * * *

Take the Bride: A Knight Brothers Novella

She used to be his. Now she's about to marry another man.
Will he let her go ... or will he stand up and take the bride?

Ryder Hammond and Sierra Knight were high school sweethearts. Despite him being her brother's best friend, their relationship burned hot and fast...and ended with heartbreak and regrets.

Years later, she's at the altar, about to marry another man.

He's only there for closure, to finally put the past behind him.

But when the preacher asks if anyone has a reason the couple shouldn't wed, she turns around and her gaze locks on his.

Suddenly he's out of his seat.

Objecting.

Claiming.

And ultimately stealing the very pissed off bride and takes her to a secluded cabin.

He wants one week to convince her they're meant to be, to remind her of the fiery passion still burning between them.

When their time together is up, will she walk away and break *his* heart this time, or will he finally have the woman he's wanted all along?

* * * *

His to Protect: A Bodyguard Bad Boys/Masters and Mercenaries Novella

Talia Shaw has spent her adult life working as a scientist for a big pharmaceutical company. She's focused on saving lives, not living life. When her lab is broken into and it's clear someone is after the top secret formula she's working on, she turns to the one man she can trust. The same irresistible man she turned away years earlier because she was too young and naive to believe a sexy guy like Shane Landon could want *her*.

Shane Landon's bodyguard work for McKay-Taggart is the one thing that brings him satisfaction in his life. Relationships come in second to the job. Always. Then little brainiac Talia Shaw shows up in his backyard, frightened and on the run, and his world is turned upside down. And not just because she's found him naked in his outdoor shower, either.

With Talia's life in danger, Shane has to get her out of town and to her eccentric, hermit mentor who has the final piece of the formula she's been working on, while keeping her safe from the men who are after her. Guarding Talia's body certainly isn't any hardship, but he never expects to fall hard and fast for his best friend's little sister and the only woman who's ever really gotten under his skin.

Just One Night
The Kingston Family Book 1
By Carly Phillips

She's the woman he can't live without.

The one he can't risk screwing up their relationship by sleeping with her.

Linc Kingston doesn't accept anything less than perfection. Not in his billion-dollar business or in his personal life. He has it all. Except one thing. His personal assistant and best friend in his bed, moaning his name. No matter how much Linc wants her, she's completely off-limits.

Jordan Greene grew up the daughter of the housekeeper at the Kingston estate, where she met and bonded with Linc at a young age, despite their economic differences. But no matter how close they are now or how much their attraction simmers beneath the surface, they're still from two different worlds. Besides, Jordan isn't about to risk losing her best friend for one sensual night.

Jordan might be the only woman who can handle Linc and his domineering, bossy attitude, but beneath that gruff exterior is a vulnerable man who, despite his wealth, has had a less-than-charmed life. And when Linc's father dies, she's there for him—unwavering in her friendship.

Until one night of passion and a positive pregnancy test changes everything.

* * * *

"I need a plan," he said, speaking up out of the blue.

She'd actually thought he'd fallen asleep.

"Do I go meet my sister? Or do I let it go because knowing the truth about her father might be too painful for her?" His tone sounded slurred and he was obviously in no position to talk tonight.

"I think we should discuss this in the morning. You need a clear head to make those kind of decisions." She pushed herself off him and rose to her feet.

"Stay with me," he said and when she glanced at him, his lips were set in a little boy pout.

This was the Linc not many people saw. The vulnerable man beneath the businessman he presented to the world. "You need sleep. Do you have a car waiting?" she asked because he used a driver to get around the city.

"I sent him home." He stretched his feet out on her couch and she realized he was settling in for the night.

"Kick off your shoes," she said. No way could he sleep on the couch in his work clothes.

He did as she instructed and his black dress shoes fell to the floor.

"Now take off your tie and shirt so you're comfortable."

"Bossy," he muttered and began undo the buttons. He worked his way down, revealing his muscled chest and defined abs from time with a professional trainer. He shrugged out of the shirt, struggling with the buttons on the cuffs but he managed to release them.

Swallowing hard, took the shirt and tie from him and put them aside, planning to hang them up so they didn't wrinkle even more. He'd need them to wear home in the morning.

Despite herself, she couldn't help but stare at his naked chest. It had been years since they were kids swimming together in his family's pool and the man in front of her now was a far cry from the boy he'd been.

How could she look at him and not drool? "Do you want to wash up before you settle in for the night?" she asked in a husky voice.

She reached a hand out to help him to his feet and without warning, he pulled her forward. She tumbled, twisting herself so she landed on top of his hard body.

"Linc, what are you doing?" She lifted herself up, intending to climb off him when a firm arm around her back locked her in place.

"I need you," he said, his voice full of longing.

His words took her off guard. Heart pounding, she looked up and his gaze, hazy with alcohol but no less compelling, met hers. Everything inside her twisted with need. Need for this man and everything he was.

"Kiss me, Jordan."

About Carly Phillips

Carly Phillips gives her readers Alphalicious heroes to swoon for and romance to set your heart on fire, and she loves everything about writing romance. She married her college sweetheart and lives in Purchase, NY along with her three crazy dogs: two wheaten terriers and a mutant Havanese, who are featured on her Facebook and Instagram. She has raised two incredible daughters who put up with having a mom as a romance author. Carly is the author of over fifty romances, and is a NY Times, Wall Street Journal, and USA Today Bestseller. She loves social media and interacting with her readers. Want to keep up with Carly? Sign up for her newsletter and receive TWO FREE books at www.carlyphillips.com.

Discover 1001 Dark Nights

Go to www.1001DarkNights.com for more information.

TRICKED by Rebecca Zanetti ~ DIRTY WICKED by Shayla Black ~ THE ONLY ONE by Lauren Blakely ~ SWEET SURRENDER by Liliana Hart

COLLECTION FOUR
ROCK CHICK REAWAKENING by Kristen Ashley ~ ADORING INK by Carrie Ann Ryan ~ SWEET RIVALRY by K. Bromberg ~ SHADE'S LADY by Joanna Wylde ~ RAZR by Larissa Ione ~ ARRANGED by Lexi Blake ~ TANGLED by Rebecca Zanetti ~ HOLD ME by J. Kenner ~ SOMEHOW, SOME WAY by Jennifer Probst ~ TOO CLOSE TO CALL by Tessa Bailey ~ HUNTED by Elisabeth Naughton ~ EYES ON YOU by Laura Kaye ~ BLADE by Alexandra Ivy/Laura Wright ~ DRAGON BURN by Donna Grant ~ TRIPPED OUT by Lorelei James ~ STUD FINDER by Lauren Blakely ~ MIDNIGHT UNLEASHED by Lara Adrian ~ HALLOW BE THE HAUNT by Heather Graham ~ DIRTY FILTHY FIX by Laurelin Paige ~ THE BED MATE by Kendall Ryan ~ NIGHT GAMES by CD Reiss ~ NO RESERVATIONS by Kristen Proby ~ DAWN OF SURRENDER by Liliana Hart

COLLECTION FIVE
BLAZE ERUPTING by Rebecca Zanetti ~ ROUGH RIDE by Kristen Ashley ~ HAWKYN by Larissa Ione ~ RIDE DIRTY by Laura Kaye ~ ROME'S CHANCE by Joanna Wylde ~ THE MARRIAGE ARRANGEMENT by Jennifer Probst ~ SURRENDER by Elisabeth Naughton ~ INKED NIGHTS by Carrie Ann Ryan ~ ENVY by Rachel Van Dyken ~ PROTECTED by Lexi Blake ~ THE PRINCE by Jennifer L. Armentrout ~ PLEASE ME by J. Kenner ~ WOUND TIGHT by Lorelei James ~ STRONG by Kylie Scott ~ DRAGON NIGHT by Donna Grant ~ TEMPTING BROOKE by Kristen Proby ~ HAUNTED BE THE HOLIDAYS by Heather Graham ~ CONTROL by K. Bromberg ~ HUNKY HEARTBREAKER by Kendall Ryan ~ THE DARKEST CAPTIVE by Gena Showalter

COLLECTION SIX
DRAGON CLAIMED by Donna Grant ~ ASHES TO INK by Carrie Ann Ryan ~ ENSNARED by Elisabeth Naughton ~

On behalf of 1001 Dark Nights,
Liz Berry, M.J. Rose, and Jillian Stein would like to thank ~

Steve Berry
Doug Scofield
Benjamin Stein
Kim Guidroz
Social Butterfly PR
Ashley Wells
Asha Hossain
Chris Graham
Chelle Olson
Kasi Alexander
Jessica Johns
Dylan Stockton
Richard Blake
and Simon Lipskar

Made in the USA
Coppell, TX
12 March 2021

51623690R00062